The Boy From N

Harry Riley, brash young reporter on a small Sussex paper, came from Brighton but he might as well have come from nowhere. He had no kin, no sense of community; what he did with his spare time was his secret. Moreover, his sneaky investigations into certain local institutions had aroused local ire. When he was found dead at the foot of a cliff, fellow reporter Sheila Tracy was one of the few to mourn him, but she never suspected his death was anything other than an accident.

Even when her suspicions were aroused, quiet respectable Seahaven seemed an unlikely venue for murder, and Sheila pursued her inquiries into Harry's life and the lives of certain local worthies with no great hopes. Then she unearthed a connection between Harry and a crime some two or three years earlier which convinced her that his death had indeed been deliberately contrived. The rest of what she unearthed was even more unexpected, and—for Sheila—deeply disturbing. Would she ever again have the same view of 'a nice place like Seahaven'?

by the same author

THE NIGHT THEY MURDERED CHELSEA
THE CORPSE NOW ARRIVING
THE TELEPHONE NEVER TELLS
ONE-WAY CEMETERY
END OF A GOOD WOMAN

MARGARET HINXMAN

The Boy From Nowhere

COLLINS, 8 GRAFTON STREET, LONDON W1

William Collins Sons & Co. Ltd
London · Glasgow · Sydney · Auckland
Toronto · Johannesburg

First published 1985
© Margaret Hinxman 1985

British Library Cataloguing in Publication Data

Hinxman, Margaret
    The boy from nowhere.—(Crime Club)
    I. Title
    823'.914[F]   PR6058.I537

ISBN 0 00 231437 1

Photoset in Linotron Baskerville by
Rowland Phototypesetting Ltd
Bury St Edmunds, Suffolk
Printed in Great Britain by
William Collins Sons & Co. Ltd, Glasgow

CHAPTER 1

'Falstaff, heel!'

Colonel Parker, retired Indian Army, was a creature of unswerving habit. Every morning he rose at seven, flung open the bedroom window, took precisely six healthy deep breaths, showered, shaved and trimmed his military moustache. Then he dressed meticulously to suit the weather, brewed a pot of best Darjeeling tea, drank two cups himself and placed another on the bedside table within handy reach of his slumbering wife.'

'Just off with Falstaff to stretch our legs, old girl' he told her unfailingly. And, unfailingly, she roused, shivered, snuggled down under the duvet and warned him drowsily not to let Falstaff consort with stray dogs, worry the neighbours' cat or otherwise disgrace himself.

Falstaff was not a creature of habit.

By eight o'clock, rain or shine, winter or summer, Colonel Parker and his self-important Scotch terrier were pacing the width of the beach underneath the overhanging cliffs that formed the cove of Seahaven. With a brisk wind slicing across from Brighton to the east, they had the beach to themselves. At exactly eight-forty-five, Colonel Parker would call Falstaff from whatever mischief he was engaged in and they would make for home.

But not this morning.

'Falstaff, heel!' the Colonel repeated.

The Scottie paused, cocked an ear, glanced dismissively at his master, then trotted purposefully off in the opposite direction towards a mound of shingle at the far end of the cove. As he approached it his stocky legs gathered speed, flicking up sprays of water from the shallow waves that lapped the shore.

'Damned dog!' the Colonel muttered, striding off in pursuit of the wayward Falstaff.

Probably a bit of driftwood that had been washed in by the tide or an interestingly smelly strip of seaweed. He checked his watch. Five minutes behind schedule. It didn't bode well for the day. Not that the day had anything particular to offer, but the Colonel still allotted his time as strictly and punctually as he did when his time meant something.

He heard the dog, having reached his target, yapping excitedly. Not like Falstaff. He might be a nuisance, but he wasn't usually a yapper.

The Colonel quickened his pace, cursing a puddle of sea-water he hadn't noticed which soaked the old-fashioned cuffs of his hardy tweed trousers.

The dog's yapping was now punctuated with growls as Falstaff stood guard over whatever trophy he had found. Within feet of him, the Colonel shook his stick and attempted another directive. 'Falstaff . . .' He never finished the command. His eyes were drawn to a heap of clothing around which Falstaff was now circling proprietorially as if warning the Colonel that it was his find.

On closer inspection the clothing took on a shape. A shape the Colonel recognized only too well from his days in combat. From the arm of a sodden anorak a lifeless hand lay bedded in the shingle, its fingers outstretched. The head, face down, was caked with blood. The Colonel noticed that one foot had lost a shoe and sock. The toes, naked, pink and wet, looked almost childlike, unformed, waiting to be born. Odd, thought the Colonel, it was always little things like that which etched the memory in the mind.

For a moment he stood, transfixed by the sight. 'Poor little blighter,' he said softly. In all his years in the service he'd never got used to the bleak ugliness of death. Then, quite deliberately, he marshalled his thoughts and shook himself into action. Falstaff looked up at him, panting expectantly, his tail wagging.

'Good boy,' said the Colonel absently. With the dog trotting obediently behind him, he strode off down the beach to call the police.

Technically, the weekly *Seahaven Telegraph* went to press on Thursday, but by Thursday morning it was all over bar the shouting. The bulk of the paper was already written and laid out, apart from a few columns on the front pages for late news. Failing the extreme unlikelihood of any startling late news, there was a report on a local charity fund-raising scheme waiting to be slotted in.

In the editorial department, Sheila Tracy idly checked the proofs of her feature on summer fashions tailored to the needs of the largely middle-aged female population of Seahaven. It had hardly been an exhilarating assignment. Seahaven women tended to favour conformity, confirmed in their opinion that real style went out when synthetics took over from natural fibres and Mary Quant invented the mini skirt.

As she had every Thursday morning for five years, Sheila asked herself the same question. What kept her here as women's page editor, churning out trivia each week and trying to make it seem new and interesting? And every Thursday morning for five years she arrived at the same answer. I'm too lethargic, too comfortable, too Seahaven to change. She recognized her own lack of ambition and had learned to live with it.

What did Stephen Gough always say? 'The trouble with you is you're too cosy. You don't want to know about the outside world. It's dark and dangerous out there.' And he was right. She doubted whether she could cope with a dark and dangerous world. Seahaven was warm and familiar. It sprang no nasty surprises. It was easier to retreat into the conviction that at thirty she was too old to branch out, to take risks with the future.

'Where the hell's that bloody boy?'

Sheila winced as Fred Happer slammed the telephone receiver down on its cradle. Fred's bark was worse than his bite but he didn't intend that anyone should ignore it.

'What bloody boy?' said Sheila, knowing very well. There was only one bloody boy in the office so far as Fred was concerned. Harry Riley.

'Who do you think? Riley was supposed to interview Jack Murray about his plans for developing the supermarket and he hasn't turned up. Murray's furious, wasted all morning . . . blah, blah, blah. I'll murder the bugger when he comes in. "Sorry, Fred, overslept, heavy night."' He mimicked Riley's insolent tone with precise accuracy.

Sheila smiled. 'Well, maybe he has overslept. I'll call his digs, if you like.'

Fred Happer ignored her offer. 'Why doesn't he get you on the raw like the rest of us? He's a nuisance, a mischief-maker, an impudent little swine . . .'

'And the best reporter the *Telegraph*'s ever had.' She relaxed in her swivel chair and pointedly fingered the keys of her typewriter. Why was it that Harry didn't make her bristle as he did everyone else, she mused. He was everything Fred said he was. But she couldn't help feeling a reluctant respect for the boy. She admired his guts, he had more spunk than the rest of them, herself included, put together. Perhaps that's why she liked him. They were so completely opposite and each in his or her way recognized the dissimilar qualities of the other.

'So he's a good reporter,' Fred conceded grudgingly. 'It's not what you do, however well, that matters here. It's how you get on with people. Stroke the local dignitaries, spell their names right and don't make waves. All the rest is a waste of time.'

'That's a condemnation of what we do.'

'Wrong. It's not a condemnation. It's a commendation. Don't knock it. You've never known Fleet Street.'

For Fred that had been a bruising experience he was

constantly examining like an old wound that had never quite healed over. He was a lumpy man in his late fifties who affected a stern brusqueness that fooled no one, least of all himself. No matter how much he cursed and ranted, the kind, deep-set eyes gave him away.

After twenty years in the editorial executive obstacle race in Fleet Street, criss-crossing from one national newspaper to another, he'd suffered a mild heart attack. It seemed barely a hiccup in a prestigious career. Other colleagues had survived much worse and returned to the race, refreshed. But in the uncustomary peace of his convalescence (even annual holidays had usually been interrupted by urgent calls from the paper), Fred had taken stock of his life. The future stretched out ahead of him, an endless stream of conferences, crises, post-mortems over scoops lost to the opposition—and, above all, panic, constant panic.

Decisively he'd written his letter of resignation. His wife had breathed a sigh of relief. His friends and associates on the Street had grieved that he would be irreplaceable, thrown him a boozy party at Scribes and vowed he'd be back. But he'd never been back. He'd settled in Seahaven, where his wife and he had a vacation bungalow, and in the fullness of time after a chance meeting with the proprietor of the *Telegraph* he'd taken the job of assistant editor. That was six years ago. By contrast with Fleet Street, it was leisurely, undemanding work. He also wrote a weekly gardening column and always reported on the annual bowls tournament, which allowed him to indulge his twin passions —growing roses and taking a turn on the bowling greens— in print.

It was a little life. Sometimes Fred felt like the man in the lobby of *Grand Hotel* who intoned: 'People come and people go, but nothing ever happens.' It suited Fred admirably.

He never mourned the future he might have had, the editorship, perhaps, of a national daily. Occasionally he heard from his old associates, but less and less as time went by. Whatever gap he'd left behind had been filled without a trace.

When Harry Riley had joined the paper barely a year before, having impressed their editor, Alec Hutchinson, with a ferrety piece he'd offered on spec about the cricket club secretary fiddling the funds, Fred had recognized a breed he knew only too well. Harry was a hustler. He thirsted for Fleet Street, for those unnerving panics, those foot-in-door triumphs.

Fred felt uncomfortable around Harry. He reminded him too much of what he'd escaped from. Even more, he reminded him of himself thirty years ago before he'd learned the cost of all that stress and strain.

Fred was not a mean man, but if there was a stray streak of meanness in him, Harry brought it out.

'I've never understood why you're so down on Harry.' It was as if Sheila Tracy had been reading his thoughts. His expression softened as he looked across at her. He always enjoyed looking at Sheila. If he were a lot younger and not happily married he'd probably have fallen in love with her. There was a serenity about her which seemed to him the most desirable quality in a woman. Everything she was was on the surface. It was a kind of beauty, though not everyone's kind of beauty. The green-grey eyes set in a neatly proportioned face regarded you frankly, without guile. The crisp, chestnut hair, already faintly flecked with grey and cut short for convenience, framed her features unobtrusively. The tall, trim figure was pleasing but not voluptuous. In a crowd she might pass unnoticed, except for the mouth. The generous lips were full of humour. You could see them savouring a joke, a silly situation, measuring the amused response they deserved before the rippling laughter they received. He wondered why she'd never married. Perhaps, after all, those frank eyes had their secrets, too.

'Penny?' She waved her hand, attracting his attention.

'Nothing. I was just thinking what an uncommonly nice woman you are.'

She grimaced in mock disgust. 'That's a killer of a thing to say to a lady of my advanced years.'

'Pure flattery, I promise.' He heaved himself out from behind his desk. 'I suppose I'd better sort out this Riley thing.'

He was aware that the office was beginning to buzz with what passed for activity at the *Telegraph*. The two secretaries were typing readers' letters. The trainee journalist who covered the Women's Institute meetings was engaged in a mildly heated conversation over the telephone with the president of one branch who was complaining about a serious omission in last week's report. The conversation was fairly one-sided.

'But Mrs Glaxton . . . yes, I know . . . it must have been a lovely lecture . . . Ming dynasty porcelain . . . we received your report, of course, but you see . . . we didn't have . . .' The girl, Molly Arkwright, looked glumly at the dead receiver in her hand. 'Space,' she concluded to no one in particular.

She was pert and pretty with a mass of spiky blonde hair which didn't endear her to the older ladies of the Women's Institute.

'Why don't they ever listen?' she asked of no one in particular. 'I kept telling her we didn't have the space.'

'Readers never listen,' said Sheila wryly. 'You'll learn that in time. Mostly, they just want you to listen.'

'Where's Harry?' the girl said without much interest. 'I was supposed to meet him at the disco in Brighton after the movie last night. He never turned up. Not that it was much of a loss. Can't stand him, really. Always touching me up.'

'I didn't know you were so thick with Harry.'

'I'm not. He's just, as they say, available. There's not a lot of talent around in Seahaven.'

'No, I suppose you're right,' said Sheila. It couldn't be

much of a life for young people. Still, there was always Brighton along the coast. No shortage of talent there.

'I did meet this super guy at the Rotary dinner dance, but he was just passing through. Said he'd get in touch.'

Sheila groaned inwardly. Molly's love-life was an unending saga that was always changing and always the same. She was about to make some soothing noise to the effect that you never knew what might be just around the corner when she noticed Fred coming out of the editor's office.

He seemed suddenly very old, weary, like a man who had taken a beating. As he stood in the centre of the room, the office became silent. The chatter ceased, the rattle of typewriter keys dried up. They looked at him expectantly. Then the figure of Alec Hutchinson, the editor, came up behind him.

'Will you tell them or shall I, Fred?'

Fred Happer shook his head.

Alec straightened his already immaculately tied tie. It was a nervous gesture that had nothing to do with vanity.

'I'm sorry to have to tell you that Harry Riley is dead. I've just spoken to the police. He was found this morning on the beach at the bottom of the cliff.'

'God! Suicide point.' It was Molly who broke their silence.

With an effort Alec contained his irritation. 'We don't know yet what happened.'

'Except he's dead. Like a drowned rat.' Fred stared directly at Sheila. There was pity in his eyes, but something else as well. Fear. His expression was so intense that she looked away. As she did so, he gasped, stumbled and fell heavily to the floor.

CHAPTER 2

'I still can't take it in.' Sheila took a sip of the brandy Alec Hutchinson had insisted on pouring for her. She closed her eyes, waiting for the mellow, relaxing after-effects. But there was no warm glow. The brandy tasted as bitter as gall.

They were sitting in Alec's office. It was long after midnight and the rest of the staff had gone home. Somehow they'd managed to put the paper to bed, without the help of Fred Happer who had been taken to the local hospital and was, according to a tart ward sister, 'as comfortable as can be expected'.

The item on the charity fund-raising scheme had been shelved and Alec had filled the late news columns with a report on Harry Riley's death, which he'd dictated with speedy precision. There was little as yet to add to the bare facts. The police were noncommittal. There would be a post mortem. As his employer, Alec had been asked to formally identify the body.

They'd fleshed out the skeletal news with several paragraphs on Colonel Parker, the much-respected resident of Seahaven who had discovered the body and offered the opinion that the cliff top was a hazard and the council were negligent in not putting up warning signs. A newly elected and eagerly available councillor had backed up the Colonel's criticism, pointing out that Harry was not the first victim to have fallen to his death off the cliff. A firmly entrenched opposition councillor had stoutly refuted claims of council negligence. 'But then, he would, wouldn't he?' Molly Arkwright had sniffed, putting into words what Alec and Sheila were too discreet or circumspect to utter.

The *Telegraph* photographer had taken a slightly out of focus picture of Colonel Parker and Falstaff not very persuasively re-enacting their discovery of the corpse. And in the centre of the front page there was a photograph of Harry Riley, which they'd dug out of the picture library.

It was a singularly unprepossessing portrait. He looked furtive, uneasy, on his marks, with his alert, ferrety eyes staring into the camera as if he were facing a firing squad. Even in repose, he seemed to be bracing himself for a hundred-yard sprint, but not as an athlete might, rather as a boy who was running out of time.

'Too bad he looks like the Artful Dodger. But it's the best we can do,' the sub editor, Roy Kennedy, had observed sourly and without much regret, before despatching the page to the printers. There'd been little love lost between him and Harry Riley.

Alec had added a grace note to the report of 'our reporter's untimely death', commenting on Harry's ingenuity, drive and promising future, now, alas, nipped in the bud. There was they all agreed, very little you could say about Harry that would make him seem endearing without being blatantly hypocritical.

In the immediate crisis of organizing the copy, interviewing interested parties and laying out the page, they'd succeeded in forgetting the cause of it. Or, at least, they'd pushed it to the back of their minds. It was turning into a good story with plenty of feedback—the cliff hazard, for example. It was only afterwards, when they'd congratulated each other on a job well done, that it had finally hit them.

Harry Riley was dead. Never again would he bounce into the office bragging about some scoop he was sure would make his name, always edgy, nervy, talking too fast out of the corner of his mouth like a junior James Cagney. He'd never belonged. He'd fitted into the comfortable atmosphere of the *Seahaven Telegraph* as threateningly as a fox in a hutchful of domestic rabbits. And now he was gone. There were those who muttered darkly that it was 'a good miss'. All the same, he would be missed.

And then there was Fred Happer's response to the news. Another mild heart attack, they'd said at the hospital. Aggravated by shock. Nothing to be alarmed about. But it was alarming, nevertheless. .

In the anti-climax after the euphoria of putting the story together and seeing it safely on to the presses, they'd shared a sense of guilt as if they'd been remiss in not paying due respect to a tragedy that, for a few hours, had been just grist to the journalistic mill.

They'd drifted off silently, leaving Sheila and Alec alone among the debris of the day. And in silence they'd nursed their brandy. She knew she'd been stating the obvious when she'd said she couldn't take it in. They were just words. But at least they broke that painful silence.

'Pity we didn't hear about the cinema sooner. We could have got that in,' said Alec. He didn't need to elaborate. A late call to the police had revealed that Harry had been last seen in the back row of a cinema in Brighton, a seedy dump incongruously named the Palace, which specialized in soft porn movies. 'I hope *Punk Lust* came up to Harry's expectations,' he chuckled, enunciating the title of the current movie, *Punk Lust*, with amused distaste.

She supposed she should find his amusement offensive in the circumstances. But Alec had the knack of putting events into perspective. Somehow the thought of Harry spending his last hours on earth watching a piece of celluloid dross called *Punk Lust* seemed appropriate. Maybe even Harry would have seen the joke. He'd had a brutal sense of humour about other people, quick-witted and occasionally lethal, such as the time he'd likened the tombstone of a late lamented mayor to a stone corpse with its toes turned up.

She sighed. 'I suppose you and I are the only people who will really mourn Harry. I can't think why I will. He was everything I rationally dislike. Brash, overbearing, impertinent, insensitive. But, I don't know, I had a feeling Harry was all right. And he made me laugh. That tombstone *does*

look like a petrified corpse with its toes turned up. What's
your excuse?'

Alec pursed his lips, seemingly giving the question serious consideration. Even at the end of a hard day he looked
freshly groomed, the tie still immaculately in place, the
toning shirt still crisp and dazzlingly clean. He wore his
forty years with a springy elegance, handsome in a slightly
saturnine way. With strangers he affected the air of a light-
weight charmer. But first appearances were deceptive. He
had, on occasion, a formidable temper and an unbudgeable
will. When he made up his mind no one could persuade him
to change it. Hiring the rogue Harry Riley had been proof
of that.

Harry had materialized like some rootless vagabond from
what Seahaven regarded as that sin city down the coast,
Brighton. He'd served restless time as a messenger boy on
the *Argus* and that was about all anyone knew about him.
He had no kin, no sense of community. In a small, close
town where everyone professed to know everything about
everyone else, what Harry did with his spare time was
Harry's secret. Even the landlady who grudgingly accepted
him as a tenant for her small furnished flatlet in Seahaven
couldn't account for his comings and goings.

The proprietor and most of the staff of the *Telegraph* had
assured Alec Hutchinson that he wouldn't fit. He'd be a
disrupting influence. But Alec had insisted. 'We need some
fresh young blood on the paper.' And he'd been proved
right. Harry may have been a menace but he was a highly
readable one. The sales had increased. People bought the
paper for the pleasure of writing outraged letters complaining about his sneaky investigations into local institutions.

Alec's answer to Sheila's question when it came was a
simple statement of fact. 'He was damned good at his job.'

'Too good sometimes.'

'Why do you say that?'

The sudden keen edge to his tone would have surprised

Sheila if it weren't that nothing Alec said or did really surprised her. The surprise was that he should remain the editor of a small-town weekly.

He was co-owner of a DIY business which had mush-roomed successfully over the years and he couldn't need the relative pittance he earned as editor. He could certainly indulge his bachelor habits—golf, sailing, Wednesday bridge—more agreeably without the added burden of run-ning a paper.

She shrugged. 'Oh—just Harry attracted trouble like the proverbial moth and flame. That series he wrote on the Wives' Guild, accusing them of being crypto Fascists, and all those hints of cover-ups and corruption in the police. Pretty hot stuff for a law and order town like Seahaven.'

'Proves my point, doesn't it? Hot stuff. Everyone read it.'

'And we almost landed ourselves with libel actions.'

'But we didn't. I monitor what our Harry writes more closely than you think.'

With the slip of tense she felt a sudden, sharp pain. Perhaps the brandy had numbed her senses.

'We're talking as if Harry were still alive.'

'Perhaps in a way he is.'

It was a bewildering thought, but there was an eerie truth in it. Everyone left behind some unfinished business. Why should Harry, of all people, be any exception?

'Why did Harry die?' The question was out almost with-out her realizing it, nonsensical and yet urgently relevant.

'How do you mean—why did he die? He died because he fell off a cliff top. I saw the body. Nothing particularly sinister. He'd certainly been drinking. That much the police could tell me straight off. Probably drugs, too. They'll know for sure after the tests.'

'What you're saying is that Harry was high, decided to go for a walk along the cliff, missed his footing and fell!'

'Or dived, when the balance . . .'

'Of his mind was affected. That's just police jargon, Alec.'

'It could also quite probably be the truth. It's not unheard of, even in Seahaven.'

'Do you want it to be true?'

'I want what you want, Sheila. The truth. Just that. I've championed Harry in the past. Even put my own job on the line for him. But he was hardly an upright citizen. Lord knows who his friends were. And he certainly couldn't come up with that item he did on the drug scene in Brighton if he weren't somehow involved with it.'

'But that doesn't make him a junkie. Oh, he probably smoked pot now and then, maybe even experimented with cocaine.'

'Well then?'

'If you think that, you don't know Harry at all, Alec. He was too astute, too in control of himself to go off half-cocked like that. Harry was an observer. He had plans, his future mapped out. He'd stay in Seahaven just so long as it suited him, then he'd be off. He may have acted like a tearaway, but only because that was the image he wanted to project. Underneath he was as single-minded as any high-powered businessman plotting a takeover deal. He'd never put his future at risk.'

She spoke with an increasing certainty, as if resolving her own doubts out loud. Lost in her thoughts, she felt a hand on her shoulder and jerked away involuntarily. Then she relaxed, realizing it was just Alec looking down at her, with a small, concerned smile.

'You've had a tough day, Sheila. We all have. Harry, then Fred. It's the wrong time for this sort of discussion. Hour of the wolf and all that.'

She returned his reassuring smile. 'You're probably right. Harry casts a mean shadow,' she conceded.

'You'll see, tomorrow, all will be made clear. We'll get the police report. Twist a few arms if we have to. Off you go. Would you like me to give you a lift?'

She shook her head. 'Thanks. But no, thanks. I've got the car outside. I do feel pretty knackered.'

She didn't realize how knackered until she got behind the wheel of her Mini Metro. She wound down the window. A touch of frost crisped the air wafting off the sea. In the distance she heard the faint rumble of traffic on the bypass. Otherwise, there was no sound to fracture the peace of sleeping Seahaven. The bright moonlight gave the carefully preserved Georgian terraces an appearance of translucent mystery.

In the morning they'd look mundane and familiar, the elegance of their architecture marred by the clutter of cars, vans and bustling pedestrians. In the morning she'd wonder why she'd ever doubted that Harry's death was anything other than a dreadful, fatal accident.

She shivered. Alec *was* right. Fertile imaginations should never be allowed to run riot during the hour of the wolf.

CHAPTER 3

Seahaven General was one of those small cottage hospitals which used to litter the country and was now constantly under threat of being phased out under the bureaucratic might of the National Health Service.

When it was built sixty years before it had been sited in the quietest part of town, nudging the South Downs, in a silver birch-lined avenue known locally as the High because of its desirable location. The large Victorian houses that flanked the High, with their important semi-circular drives and landscaped gardens, had been much sought after between the wars by the wealthy burghers and professional men of Seahaven. But even in a town where change seemed imperceptible, they were an anachronism which couldn't survive inflation, the disappearance of domestic servants, the industrial development of the surrounding area and the greedy speculation of the property developers.

One by one the Victorian monstrosities—for indeed they were æsthetically monstrous—had been sold off and bull-dozed, causing a particularly acrid local controversy about the blight of 'in-filling'. In their place maisonettes, two-storeyed blocks of flats and small town houses, aping the genuine Georgian proportions of the terraces in the centre of old Seahaven, had been crammed cheek by jowl into plots of land whose every inch had been carefully planned to conform to the minimum requirements of the building regu-lations. The silver birches had been retained, giving the High a glancing elegance which belied the unimaginative uniformity of the dwellings they now guarded.

Only the hospital remained as a bastion of the past, proudly intimidating the cramped flats and town houses crouched on either side of it. It had an air of defiance about it which was well founded. Seahaven General's days were numbered. It was only a matter of time before its function would be parcelled out to the far larger, better equipped and staffed Brighton or Worthing hospitals.

Meanwhile it operated as it always had done, like a corporate family doctor whose treatment tended to be based more on familiarity with the patient's history of illness than on exact science. Its small, light wards gave off an atmosphere of peace and well-being.

If you had to be ill, thought Sheila, as she nosed the car into the visitors' parking area, you could hardly pick a more agree-able place to be ill in than Seahaven General. Although she doubted whether Fred Happer would agree. The telephone call from his wife had awakened her from a restless sleep punctuated by nightmare dreams of Harry Riley plunging, screaming, off a cliff which wasn't in Seahaven, but in some strange, futuristic fantasy land like a set design for *Star Wars*.

Mabel Happer had sounded worried, which she supposed was natural, but there was an urgency in her voice that her

simple statement 'Fred would like to see you' didn't seem
to warrant.

She was waiting for Sheila in the reception area of the
main hospital, set apart from the outpatients' department.
It was only 9.30 and official visiting hours were from 11.0
to 12.0, but like everything else at Seahaven General visiting
hours were flexible. She was sitting bolt upright on a bench
across from the porter's office, her squat body tensed unnatu-
rally as if bracing itself for bad news.

When she spotted Sheila her anxious face relaxed momentarily.

'I'm so glad you're here. I'm sorry I called you. So early.
I know what it's like after press day. But Fred was so
insistent. That is, he *seemed* to be.' There was the same
worried urgency in her voice that Sheila had detected over
the telephone.

Sheila put her arm round the small, taut body. 'But he's
all right, isn't he? Fred. They said it was nothing to be
alarmed about.'

'Not really. I wish they weren't so—so soothing here. I
wish they'd tell you straight away. It was late last night. He
took a turn for the worse. He's quite conscious. But it's
obviously more serious than they thought at first.

'It's just he kept asking for you. And I felt if only he could
see you and say whatever it was on his mind, he could rest
easy.'

Sheila found herself groping for reassuring words which
might comfort the distraught woman. 'I'm sure it's nothing.
Probably something silly about the office. You know how
little things prey on his mind.'

'I thought all this was over, Sheila. All the worry. When
he left Fleet Street. And it was over until that boy came to
the paper. Just little niggles at first. He never liked Harry
Riley, you know. It's dreadful to say it, now that he's dead.'

Sheila sighed. 'He wasn't alone. Harry wasn't much liked
I'm afraid.'

'All the same, he put up with him, even admired him, I think. But in the last few weeks when he came home I could tell he was concerned about something more than just the usual irritations. He wouldn't tell me, said he wasn't even sure himself why he should be concerned. He started getting those pains in the chest again, but I couldn't make him see the doctor. You know what men are.'

'Perhaps we should go and see Fred now.'

The little woman seemed consciously to pull herself to-gether at the prospect of some positive action. 'The ward sister said we could have a few minutes. It's a very nice room and they're all so kind.' She emphasized the qualities of the hospital as if convincing herself that niceness and kindness might keep her husband alive.

A brisk young nurse led the way, expatiating about what a good patient Mr Happer was and how necessary it was that he shouldn't be taxed in any way. Nothing in her tone prepared Sheila for the drastic change she saw in Fred as he lay propped up on pillows in the narrow hospital bed. His face was gaunt and grey, although he mustered the semblance of a smile and lifted a limp hand of welcome as she took a seat beside his bed. She cursed herself for not thinking to pick up some flowers on the way.

'Good of you,' he whispered. 'Paper go to press?'

She started to say something comforting and useless to the effect that he'd soon be up and about, but the weary look in his eyes begged her not to waste time on trivia.

'It's about Harry.' His voice was barely audible and Sheila had to lean forward to hear him clearly, although Mabel Happer, standing anxiously by the window plucking the folds of the gaudily striped curtain, caught his drift immediately.

'Fred, you know what the doctor said.'

'Don't fuss, Mabel.' His voice was stronger now with a touch of irritation, more like Sheila remembered. Whatever he wanted to say he was determined to say it, doctor or no doctor.

'What about Harry?' Sheila took his hand in hers. It felt soft, yielding, in her own cool fingers.

'I think he was on to something. More dangerous than I realized at the time.'

'When . . . ?'

He cut short her interruption.

'You know what he was like, always beavering away. A couple of days ago I came on him in the basement poring over old copies of the paper. I must have caught him by surprise. He turned round and I'll never forget the look of triumph in his eyes. He should have been on a job and I bawled him out. He just laughed. And that made me more angry. He said I was a fool. Me, a Fleet Street man and I hadn't even spotted a headline story under my nose.'

He paused, motioned towards the side table and a jug of barley water. He eased himself up awkwardly and drank thirstily from the glass of cloudy liquid Sheila poured for him, then settled himself back on the pillows, breathing heavily. She waited patiently until the panting subsided.

'I was furious. Not at what he said, but at his manner. He could always get me on the raw. Couldn't be bothered with his piddling little *exposés*. He could find something sinister about Tesco's selling more Brooke Bond than Tetley teabags.'

He attempted a grin at his own feeble joke and Sheila realized they'd relieved him of his dentures. It seemed a mean trick to play on a man's dignity, however necessary.

'But then, when they found him dead, it hit me. Sheila, I think maybe Harry was murdered. No proof, no evidence. Only a feeling that maybe this time he wasn't just bragging. Maybe he had unearthed something we were all too close to to recognize. I shouldn't burden you with this, except I know you cared about him in a funny way.'

'Did you tell anyone else?'

'No. No one but you. Because, don't you see, Sheila, if he had stumbled on a well-kept secret it has to involve someone or some group in Seahaven. If they were prepared to get rid of Harry, they'd also be prepared . . .'

'Fred, I can't believe all this.'

'Neither can I, logically. But in my bones I do. Perhaps, after all, you can take the man out of Fleet Street but you can't take Fleet Street out of the man.' Another half-hearted grin, exposing those pathetic, naked gums. Then he tightened his grip on her hand with surprising firmness.

'Sheila, all I'm saying is keep your eyes and ears open. If there's someone you feel you can trust, confide in, then go ahead. But be very sure. Because if I'm right, if Harry was murdered, whoever did it must have carried a lot of clout in Seahaven to cover up the story as long as they have.'

'But even if you're right, Fred, it could just have been one of the ravers he hung about with in Brighton, an argument, a fight. The police will find that out.'

'Maybe, maybe not.' The tension drained out of his hollow face. 'I feel better now, knowing you know. Just one other thing. Harry used to keep a notebook, sort of diary, very protective about it.'

'I remember.' The memory of that shabby black diary suddenly flashed into her mind. She couldn't think why she'd forgotten it. Harry had made such a thing about his notebook.

'Try to find it. It might give you a lead. But be careful.'

The brisk nurse popped her head round the door. 'Five minutes is up,' she said brightly. 'Doctor's on his way.'

Fred's hand slackened its grip. For a moment Sheila remained seated, staring into the exhausted eyes of the man in the bed, until she felt Mabel Happer's light touch on her arm.

'We'd better go.' She still sounded concerned, but also rather cross, as if Sheila were now an interloper who'd stolen precious minutes that belonged rightly to herself and her ailing husband.

'Come along, please. Can't keep doctor waiting.' It was the nurse's final demand, not to be ignored. Keeping doctor waiting was the cardinal crime in the nursing manual.

'Sheila!' She turned on the point of leaving at the sound of that faint voice from the bed. 'Sheila! I'm sorry.'

She nodded reassuringly. 'Don't worry, Fred. It's all right.'

But it wasn't all right. She knew what Fred meant. He was sorry for unloading on her the burden of his own suspicion. He was sorry for all her quiet hours which wouldn't be quiet any more until she'd proved him positively right or wrong. He was sorry for shattering her illusions about the nice, peaceful, law-abiding town and the nice, peaceful, law-abiding citizens she'd known all her life.

She told herself she was glad that she'd made him feel easier, just talking out his fears. But she knew she resented his confidences, perhaps because they confirmed her own niggling doubts about Harry's death.

'Did you hear any of that?' she asked Mabel Happer, once they were outside.

'I didn't want to hear and I don't want to hear,' she replied tartly. 'That boy's done enough damage. I'm glad he's dead and I don't care how he died. I just want Fred to get well.'

From her tone Sheila realized she'd not only dismissed the subject, she was totally erasing it from her mind.

'You'll let me know. How Fred goes on. I'll visit, of course.'

'Perhaps it would be better if you didn't. He's said his say.' Then she seemed to relent. 'Sheila, I don't want him bothering about this—this obsession any more. The doctor spoke about a by-pass operation. But he's got to be stronger before they can attempt it. The less he sees and hears of the office the better. You do see, don't you?'

'Yes, I can see. I'll tell them at the paper that it's better he doesn't have visitors for a while.'

'I hate newspapers,' the woman said bitterly. 'I always have. But I never thought of the *Telegraph* as a newspaper, not in the way I mean. It was just a quiet retiring job, no problems, no strain. But it doesn't matter whether it's a local weekly or a national, they're all the same—in the end.'

'I suppose you're right. In the end. I'd never thought about it either.'

It was true, she hadn't. Only now it wasn't just dark and dangerous in the outside world, as Stephen Gough had warned her. It had become dark and dangerous right here where she lived.

Suddenly, she longed to talk to Stephen, to mine his incisive intelligence and his shrewd outsider's powers of observation. Stephen would make sense of it all, blow away the cobwebs, ridicule the alarm her visit to Fred had generated.

As she drove back to the office, she debated whether she should telephone him, even though the last time they'd met she'd sworn never to see that self-satisfied, opinionated cynic again.

CHAPTER 4

Andrew Tracy was busy in the potting shed at the rear of the trim, gabled house on the outskirts of Seahaven which he shared with his daughter when Sheila returned from the hospital. He was a large, beefy man whose weathered face and muscular build suggested a lifetime of outdoor manual labour. It came as a surprise to those who didn't know him that he'd spent all his working years in the local branch of Barclays Bank from which he'd retired as manager two years before, at the early age of sixty.

The huge hands, which seemed fashioned for bricklaying, fondled the fragile fuchsias he was considering planting out with amazing tenderness.

'You were up early.' The voice, soft, well-modulated, belied his appearance. He didn't look up, sensing Sheila's presence without needing to convince himself that she was there. The close relationship they'd developed over the years since the death of his wife when Sheila was a child had built up a kind of cosy telepathy between them based on mutual affection and a necessary regard for each other's privacy.

The smile she directed at the enormous, grey-haired head bent over the delicate plants indicated the deep love she had for this lion of a man who had been father and mother to her for almost as long as she could remember.

'I went to see Fred in hospital.' She hadn't seen her father since the previous morning when she'd left for the office. He'd been in bed when she'd returned in the small hours and a hasty phone call was the only time she was able to steal from the hectic day to fill him in on the events that had cast a gruesome shadow over the orderly serenity of her life.

'Not bad news, I hope.' For the first time he turned to face her.

'Not particularly good either.'

He touched her cheek with his great paw. She looked drawn and worried.

'Talk about it later. What'll it be? Toast and coffee or the full works?'

She hadn't thought about food for almost twenty-four hours and she suddenly realized how hungry she was.

'Full works,' she decided firmly.

As he deftly organized the bacon and eggs, sliced bread and percolated the coffee, she found herself pouring out the whole story, Harry's death, Fred's reaction, her conversation with Alec. Gradually her own fears infiltrated into her recital of the bald, alarming facts. Andrew listened silently, nodding now and then, until he placed the plate of hot food in front of her and poured a mug of coffee.

'Eat up,' he ordered. 'You'll think more clearly on a full stomach.' She needed no urging. Ravenously she attacked the crisp bacon and eggs sunny side up just as she liked them, the yolks seeping into a sinful slice of fried bread.

She was aware of his watching concern as she ate, relishing the comfort of his protective understanding. When she finally placed the knife and fork on the empty plate, she sat back and sighed.

'I always said you'd make a good short order cook.'

'Well, we old pensioners sometimes have our uses.'

She wondered, not for the first time, what she'd do without him, resolutely dismissing the obvious afterthought that some day she would have to do without him.

'So, what are you going to do?' he asked.

'Do I have a choice?'

'You could just forget what Fred told you about Harry, write off the boy's death as a tragic accident. Go on as you've been going on.'

'Head in sand. Little Dolly Daydream believing the best of everyone in the best of all possible worlds.' She knew very well that her father's feeling about her craving for a quiet, limited life with no jagged edges coincided closely with that of Stephen Gough.

'Something like that.'

She eyed him shrewdly. 'But you don't think I should.'

'Have I ever presumed to tell you what you should do? Well, lately, that is.'

'No,' she admitted. 'But you usually manage to make it pretty plain what you think without words.'

'Sheila, if you want to know what I think, I don't believe you want my advice at all. You're just using me as a sounding-board. You made up your mind when you left the hospital—or maybe sooner, when you heard that Harry Riley was dead and something told you it wasn't quite as

cut and dried as all that—that he didn't deserve to die
without a little attention being paid. All the same, I don't
want to see you . . .' He paused as if unsure how to phrase
what he wanted to say or, perhaps, whether he should say
it at all.

'What don't you want?'

He patted her hand. 'Nothing. Just take it easy. You're
better than you think, my girl. By the way, Steve wants you
to call him, wondered if you were free for dinner tonight.
Could do worse than chat it over with him.'

'When did you hear from Steve?' she said guardedly. It
was as if he had anticipated her sudden resolve to swallow
her pride and contact Steve, despite the prickly atmosphere
of their last meeting.

'Came over last night. We played a cut-throat game of
chess and put the world to rights. You're not the only
attraction in this household, I'll have you know.'

The mocking words were matched by a sly smile. He was
always needling her about Stephen Gough, regarding their
battles of words and wits as a particularly enjoyable spectator sport. Except, Sheila thought ruefully, she was usually
outwitted and Stephen was better with words.

'You encourage him,' she bit back. The accusation had
little to do with chummy evenings and cut-throat games of
chess, but they both knew what she meant.

'And don't tell me it's a pity I don't encourage him,
because it's none of your business and I wish you wouldn't
stir it up,' she countered, before he'd even uttered.

It was the one subject that ruffled her normal serenity,
arousing a truculence in her that was out of character. Only
to herself did she admit that Steve unnerved her. He always
had from the first time she'd met him when she'd interviewed
him for a feature in the *Telegraph*. He'd been a foreign
correspondent for a national newspaper when a book he'd
written about the Falklands War had been published at the
right moment and hit the bestseller lists. From the proceeds

of that lucky break he'd given up journalism, bought himself a pleasant wreck of a cottage a few miles from Seahaven, renovated it and settled down to a hobby, science fiction, he'd previously had to sacrifice to the necessity of earning a living. The bizarre fantasies he wrote baffled Sheila as much as the man himself.

He had the reputation of being something of a recluse yet he took a lively, if cynical, interest in the mini-dramas of the small town he'd adopted. He'd led, she assumed, a hectic and high-powered life in London and abroad, but he didn't appear to miss it. He derided his temporary celebrity as a bestselling author, preferring the relative anonymity he enjoyed as a writer who reliably churned out a book every six months which pleased him and just enough loyal S.F. readers to provide him with an adequate income and keep his publishers happy.

His private life was a mystery and she knew only that he was divorced. He didn't talk much about his past work, as if scratching the scars he'd received from observing the injustices and horrors in the trouble spots of the world would have been too painful an exercise.

The edginess of their relationship had been apparent during that first interview when she'd arrived with her notebook and ballpoint and a bland set of questions and ended up with a flea in her ear and an invitation to go sailing with him the next Sunday.

Unlike most of the men in Seahaven she knew, who tended to treat women as helpless creatures, lovable for all their faults, he goaded her into taking issue with him, challenging her standards, her morality, her complacency. He seemed to take special delight in arousing her wrath, then complimenting her on losing her cool.

'I half expect you to tell me I'm gorgeous when I'm angry,' she told him wearily after one particularly fractious exchange.

'Not gorgeous,' he'd said dismissively, 'you're not the

gorgeous type. Just more interesting. You've a good mind and you've just let it lie fallow.'

And sometimes she admitted to herself that he stretched her mind as no man had ever done before or anyone else for that matter. Except perhaps her father.

It was a constant source of amazement to her that he and Steve had hit it off from the beginning when she'd nervously asked him to lunch one Sunday. Andrew, who'd barely strayed outside Seahaven except for the war, high days and holidays, and the newspaperman who'd hardly ever known a settled existence had achieved an instant rapport which mystified her.

She suspected that Andrew saw him as a likely suitor for his daughter and the unspoken thought was a bone of contention between them.

Her friends, she knew, although no one was so indelicate as to say so, were convinced she'd never married because she felt it her duty to stay with Andrew. It was a belief she didn't discourage because it relieved her of the necessity of examining her own motives for not marrying. There had, after all, been several proposals. But not lately. In Seahaven she was now regarded as not the marrying kind.

It was Andrew who was always urging her to take the plunge. 'If I ever thought I was preventing you from being a wife, a mother or taking a trip to the moon if you felt like it, I'd never forgive myself. And if you thought that, I'd never forgive *you*,' he'd once told her in one of those rare moments when they revealed their deepest feelings to each other.

She'd laughed it off, making some idiot remark about chance being a fine thing, but he hadn't been convinced.

She watched him neatly stacking the plates and scouring the frying-pan. She couldn't leave him on an angry word.

'I like my life just as it is.'

He turned round, scourer in hand, dripping washing-up liquid on the kitchen floor. 'Sheila, you don't *have* a life. You just think you do. Maybe it's me, maybe we should have got out of this place when your mother died. If I didn't know you better I'd think you were scared of being your own person.'

'I am scared,' she said quietly, 'I'm scared of the dark, of the unexpected, of responsibility, of aiming for something I can't achieve. But you *do* know me well enough for that. And I cover it up pretty convincingly. Only now I'm scared of this whole rotten business over Harry. And that's something else.'

He put his arm awkwardly around her shoulders. 'I know. I know. But there's a moment of truth in everyone's life. Maybe this is yours. I let mine go, I didn't even recognize it, when I turned down the chance to go to Canada after the war.'

'But that was Mother, I always thought.'

'No, it wasn't. It was me. I was scared. A different sort of scared to what you're feeling now. But it all adds up to the same thing in the end.' He shook himself free of that long-ago memory. 'Call Steve. He cares about you, you know.'

'Even though he's got funny ways of showing it.' She held up her hands in mock surrender. 'I will. I'll call him.'

She picked up her briefcase purposefully. 'Into battle.'

'But take it easy,' he warned.

'That's rich, coming from you. I've got this Festival meeting this evening so I'll probably be late. And by the way, if you want my opinion about the fuchsias . . .'

'I don't.'

'It's too early to plant them out. There was a nip in the air last night.'

'Get off with you, girl. You look after your piddling little newspaper, I'll look after the garden.'

As she walked briskly down the drive and slid behind the wheel of her car she thought about the night before and the fears she'd had as she drove through the quiet, empty streets. In the sparkling sunlight they didn't seem so menacing, but they were still there.

CHAPTER 5

The receptionist in the cubicle that led into the *Telegraph* offices was doggedly unravelling a puce-coloured sweater, winding the yarn into a skein round her arm while considering a knitting pattern in a woman's magazine.

A sullen girl with a pasty complexion that didn't tone harmoniously with puce, Daphne Walters looked up unsmiling as Sheila came through the door.

'They say double knit. Do you think if I used bigger needles it would make up in four ply?'

'Shouldn't think so. Best to stick to the wool they recommend.'

The girl sighed. 'That's what I thought too. Awful about Harry,' she said, almost as an afterthought. Daphne was not renowned for wasting words on a *fait accompli*. Dead was dead and no *fait* could be more *accompli* than that.

'Funny chap. Always asking questions, secretive like. Ever heard of someone called Stride?'

The name rang a distant bell but brought no instant memory to mind. Sheila shook her head, but tucked the thought into her mental filing cabinet.

'Me neither. He asked a week or so ago, like I was supposed to know or something.' She contemplated the profusion of puce straddling her arm distastefully. 'I'd better find a four ply pattern then.'

Or, better yet, ditch the puce four ply and start again, thought Sheila. 'Anyone in?'

'You're the first.'

With relief Sheila surveyed the empty office. With luck she'd be left to herself for an hour before the rest of the *Telegraph* staff drifted in, traditionally allowing themselves the luxury of being late the morning after press day.

Stephen Gough answered her telephone call in his usual clipped, urgent manner, which didn't deter her. After years as a newspaperman he still regarded the telephone as a necessary instrument of torture, strictly for business.

His voice softened slightly as he realized the caller was Sheila.

'I gather you had a busy day.' The understatement was equally typical of him and she knew him well enough by now to realize he was merely trying to lighten the burden of her own anxiety.

'You could say that,' she replied, taking her tone from his. 'Stephen . . .'

'I hope you're not going to apologize for calling me a self-satisfied, opinionated cynic.'

'I wouldn't dream of it. You are. But just, as they say, at this moment in time I could use a little opinionated cynicism.'

'God! The clichés you pick up from television.' She could picture the indulgent smile easing the lines of tension in a face that always reminded her of a patrician Alsatian whose pedigree had been polluted somewhere along the line by a pugnacious bulldog. 'What about dinner?'

'Sorry, it'll have to be late. Unless, that is, you'd like to come along to the meeting of the Festival committee first. I promised Alec I'd write it up now that Harry . . .' She left the sentence trailing awkwardly.

'Now that Harry is dead,' he finished it for her firmly. Full stop. Dead. 'You really liked that awful little pusher, didn't you.' It wasn't a question. 'Well, maybe it'll be educational watching the worthies of Seahaven putting forward their vested interests in promoting the town as a centre of jollification and harmony.' His comment was deliberately sardonic. The annual bank holiday Seahaven Festival in August was noted for causing more local acrimony than any other event in the town's calendar.

'You really are a pill, Steve. But yes, it probably will be educational, and yes, I'd like you to come.'

'And just maybe it will give you a line on why Harry died.' Like her father, he had an uncanny knack of predicting her motives before she'd actually formulated them herself. It was a *trait* that both pleased and angered her.

This morning of all mornings it angered her. But she controlled her irritation with a curt 'Then that's settled. Seven. At the White Hart.'

'Well, at least we can get a decent meal there afterwards.'

'I'd rather not,' she said quickly. 'Somewhere not quite so public.'

'Ah. Secrets.' Again she imagined that light, teasing smile. 'Maybe.'

For what seemed a long while but was probably only five minutes she sat in her familiar chair at her familiar desk enjoying the unnatural quiet of the office and the satisfaction of having nerved herself to phone Steve. She was more glad than she cared to admit that he'd instinctively sensed her concern. When she'd left the hospital after seeing Fred she'd felt desperately alone, the recipient of a confidence that couldn't be shared. But now she had an ally. Or, at least, a Devil's advocate she could trust. For all his infuriating faults Steve was an outsider, cool and objective. To him, Seahaven was merely an agreeable place to live, not a way of life. She'd never questioned that way of life before, never suspected that the people—the neighbours, colleagues and friends—she'd taken for granted for years might be more or less than the image of themselves they projected. If Fred were right, Harry Riley had discovered a flaw in that comforting façade, a flaw so ugly it might have cost him his life.

On the other hand it might just be Harry imagining he'd found the scoop that would be his passport to a nebulous fame and freedom.

'Once I get going there'll be no stopping me. Fleet Street. That's just the beginning. Harry Riley. Top TV investigator. *World in Action*. Maybe I'll get my own show. Trial by Television. David Frost did it. Why not me?'

She could hear that cocky young voice as clearly as if he were perched on her desk, as he invariably did at the end of the day, rocking back and forth, his wiry frame twitching with nervous energy.

She'd studied him with amusement, indulging his fantasies. He hadn't seemed to mind the hostility he'd aroused. Maybe it had merely reinforced the contempt he had for those who didn't share his burning ambition. Sheila didn't kid herself that the soft spot he evidently had for her had anything to do with affection. She was just the funnel through which he could let off steam.

'Sheil.' He'd managed to find a diminutive or a nickname, usually derisive, for everyone. 'Sheil, you ought to get off your butt and do something with your life.' His language owed much to the jargon of American movies, just as his impression of a hot-shot reporter was fashioned by the heroes of improbable newspaper yarns.

'I don't want to get off my butt and do something and I don't like being called Sheil.' It had never been an unkindly rebuff. But it had usually meant: end of conversation. Then with an absurdly furtive gesture he'd bring out that scruffy diary of his and, while no one else appeared to be watching in the office, he'd 'bury the evidence' as he put it.

Bury the evidence! She'd always thought it was only a little black book of addresses, available girlfriends or would-be girlfriends. Now she wasn't so sure, any more than Fred had been.

And, she knew, behind Harry's gaudy gaucheness, whether assumed or genuine, there had lurked an incisive brain, an ability to learn fast and assemble facts.

Resolutely she applied her mind to remembering where he hid the diary that had seemed so precious to him. He wouldn't keep it at his digs, when he wasn't at the office. He hadn't trusted his landlady not to pry into his sparse possessions, with good enough reason. She was a notorious snooper. If he'd had it with him, they'd presumably have found it when his body was discovered.

Think, think, woman, she told herself briskly. Until now the fact of his death had clouded the trivia of his living. Remember the little things! The way he used to bite the end of his ballpoint when he was searching for a word. The habit he had of cradling the telephone receiver in the crook of his neck when he was taking a call because that's how he'd seen Robert Redford do it in *All The President's Men*. The manner in which he pounded a typewriter as if his life depended on it.

She swung round in her swivel chair, conjuring up a mental picture of Harry around the office, breathing down Fred Happer's neck as he leafed through his copy, chatting up Molly Arkwright, leaning against the filing cabinets with that smirky grin when he knew he'd turned in a good story.

Suddenly the right image clicked into place.

'What's so interesting about the obituary file?' she'd asked him once.

'Isn't that where all the bodies are buried?' he'd replied. And then: 'Poor old X, it must get lonely, no one has a surname beginning with an X.'

'Unless you count Xerxes or Xenophon,' she'd laughed, not really paying much attention to him.

He looked at her, puzzled, apparently never having heard of the King of Persia and the Greek historian, BC.

'Anyway, what's so special about the X's?'

'Nothing.' His tone had been curiously curt and final as if he'd wished he hadn't brought up the subject. If she'd bothered to think about it, it was a strange reaction from Harry who could spin out a silly discussion to the point of screaming boredom.

And she hadn't bothered to think about it—until now.

Time was pressing. Very soon the staff of the *Seahaven Telegraph* would be coming into the office and if the diary was to be found she didn't want anyone else around when

she found it. She couldn't explain to herself the need for
secrecy and, in these familiar surroundings, she now
doubted whether Fred's warning to 'be careful' had been
anything more than the anxiety of a sick man. All the
same, she couldn't forget the look in his eyes which had so
disturbed her in that instant between his hearing of Harry's
death and keeling over on the office floor.

Swiftly, she opened the top drawer of Fred's desk and
took the key to the filing cabinet from its accustomed place
under the pocket Oxford dictionary. She noticed that her
hands were trembling as she unlocked the cabinet and rifled
through the bulging obituary folders. By comparison with
the dog-eared 'B's 'H's and 'M's, much used and hastily
handled, the 'X' folder was clean and pristine. It contained
one meagre page testifying to the fact that a long-forgotten
local insurance broker, whose main claim to fame had been
his unlikely surname 'Xylos', had died peacefully at the age
of 93 in a rest home for the aged in 1922.

Tucked behind the few respectful paragraphs on the life
of Albert Xylos, deep in the recess of the folder, her fingers
located a slim notebook. She withdrew it hastily, recognized
the scuffed black moroccon binding. For a moment she
remained squatting on the floor, handling the diary which
had suddenly become as important to her as it had been to
Harry.

Then she glanced over her shoulder as she heard a sound
from the outside office. It was only Daphne idling away the
dead time by phoning a friend whose own time supposedly
was weighing just as heavily. The faint drone of idle chatter
restored her sense of humour.

She chuckled quietly to herself, at herself, for behaving
like a trainee Miss Marple caught in the act of uncovering
the villain. After all, this was Seahaven, wasn't it? Dastardly
deeds weren't done in Seahaven. This was the office she'd
inhabited every week of her working life since she'd been
taken on as a shorthand typist at the age of 18. The people

who would walk through that editorial door were as unlikely to be mixed up in murder as any of the nice or pompous, intelligent or fatuous residents she interviewed for her column.

She'd be getting as bad as Harry, seeing mysteries in every veiled glance, every unfinished statement off the record.

Nevertheless, she slipped the diary into the pocket of her skirt, closed and locked the filing cabinet and restored the key to Fred's top drawer. She noticed that her tights had laddered and reminded herself to buy a new pair in her lunch-hour.

She tried to concentrate on the forthcoming Festival committee meeting, what questions she should ask, what line Alec would want her to take on the proceedings, whether the faint rumblings of some local traders that it was an expense the town could do without in these days of rate cutbacks should be discounted or given some weight. She imagined the committee sipping orange juice before thankfully falling on the harder stuff at the White Hart. The self-important Lester Barnes, the proprietor of the White Hart, who represented the local chamber of commerce; George Lacey, bluff and easy-going, Alec Hutchinson's partner in the DIY business; Inspector Jimmy Grant of the local police, monitoring the madder suggestions that might, if adopted, disrupt the traffic and cause an affray.

And all the others with their private axes to grind. Marion Blythe, the chairwoman of the Wives' Guild, chairpersons weren't recognized in Seahaven, who would surely veto any proposal that involved half-clad girls on floats. Her husband, Edgar, who was a solicitor and town councillor and, Sheila suspected, not as hen-pecked as he appeared. Sane, sensible John Agnew, the surveyor and Rotarian, who could be counted on to trade angry words with the brash property developer Jack Murray. Mrs Ida Glaxton, who would certainly side in most matters with Marion Blythe unless the interests of the Women's Institute were threatened; she

would also speak up for the Seahaven Musical Comedy
Society of which she was a founder member. Dr Bile, who
always seemed determined to live up to his unfortunate
name. And Mrs Eleanor Rushton, the widow of indetermi-
nate age, whose good works for charity and, even more, her
position as a member of the landed gentry, entitled her to
a seat on every committee.

Sheila felt she could write the report without even attending the meeting. It would all be so predictable.

She made a few notes on her typewriter. But her mind
wasn't on the subject. It kept darting back to the diary she'd
lifted from the file. Although she'd promised herself not to
study it until later, she took it out of her pocket and flicked
through the pages. At first sight they made little sense.
Harry's handwriting was appalling, the result of a misspent
boyhood in school.

Then her eyes alighted on a thickly underlined entry
written in a clearer, bolder hand. 'Es really low today. I
promised her I wouldn't let the bastard get away with
it.' The writing became more muddled as if expressing
half-formed thoughts. 'Bastard or bastards? Not sure yet.
Cover up? Poor Mart!'

'That's what I like to see, an eager reporter.' The unexpected voice startled her. She hadn't heard Alec come in and
instinctively she stuffed the notebook back in her pocket,
hoping he hadn't seen it.

CHAPTER 6

Turning down an invitation to lunch at the neighbouring
pub with Roy Kennedy, chief sub cum *Telegraph* soccer
correspondent, Sheila bought herself a sheltered nook in the
public gardens that nestled in the centre of town like a
boutonnière on a lapel.

With its graceful little memorial to the Warrior Birds of World War II and its border of herbs specially planted for the blind, who could finger the leaves and smell the fragrance, it was a charming haven of peace and quiet which always restored her faith in the fundamental decency of people. Any town which cared so much about the pigeons who 'gave their lives on active service' carrying messages across the Channel during the war and the blind who weren't able to see the flowers the sighted take for granted couldn't be rotten at the core.

But today she had no time or inclination to enjoy the contented atmosphere, to watch the elderly nodding off in the late spring sunshine on seats donated by relatives to the memory of some dear departed father or mother, to relish the laughter of children playing hide-and-seek round the shrubs and borders.

The ham sandwich lay ignored beside her as she leafed through the pages of Harry's diary. It was a curious jumble of dates, appointments and random jottings, most of which could only have made sense to Harry. Reminders of office assignments, interviews, Council meetings, etc., were mixed in with trivial comments on the current state of Harry's love-life—'M.A. dead boring' (Molly Arkwright wouldn't take kindly to that, thought Sheila)—and capsule judgements on his colleagues. Sheila was amused to see that in a rating of one to ten she—'S.T.—' was awarded eight. 'Classy lady, too laid back.' Added to this assessment was an odd footnote: 'can trust'.

Ambivalent remarks were attached to initials, some of which she could translate into names but not many. 'Met J.S. Not good but cheap. Best I can afford.' Who the hell could J.S. be and what was the best Harry could afford? she wondered. On the day before he died when Fred had found him poring over the old *Telegraph* files in the library one word was written boldly: 'Bullseye!'

As a source of information about what Harry had been

up to in the weeks before his death, the diary seemed a dead loss to her. No doubt Harry would have been able to unravel his own cryptic messages but he'd wrapped them up so carefully it was obvious that he didn't intend anyone else to decode them.

Only that underlined entry she'd first seen in the office before being interrupted by Alec's arrival spoke with any kind of clarity. It was as if Harry had been too disturbed or concerned to bother about caution. 'Es really low today.' 'If only Mart'd had a better lawyer.' In his customary fashion Harry didn't name names. But 'Es' and 'Mart' surely had to be abbreviations of christian names. And who were they and the 'bastard' or 'bastards'? The last entry was plain enough. 'Palace cinema 8.0 p.m.' No mystery there.

Nothing in the diary seemed to provide a clue to the questions it raised. She was beginning to doubt whether the questions were even worth answering. 'Can trust' he'd written about her. Trust to make a fool of herself bothering about the ramblings of a dead boy who'd just wanted to convince himself he was cleverer than the rest of them.

As she slipped the diary into her shoulder-bag, she was aware of a shadow blocking the pocket of sunlight in which she'd been basking. She looked up abruptly into the friendly eyes of George Lacey.

'Sorry, if I made you jump.'

'You didn't,' she said more curtly than she meant, wondering how long he'd been standing behind her.

He didn't seem to notice her sharp tone.

'Taking a breather?'

'I like to come here when the weather's decent, get away from the office and watch the world go by.' It was only a small lie.

'So do I.'

She relaxed a little. She liked George Lacey, although the amiable business relationship between this avuncular,

earthy man and the smoothly elegant Alec Hutchinson had
always surprised her. She supposed that each recognized
the qualities of the other partner: George ran the practical
side of their company efficiently while Alec handled the
public relations. And, to his credit, the latter had never
allowed the business to interfere with or influence his judgements as editor of the *Telegraph*. Indeed it wasn't until he
was firmly entrenched in the editorial chair that anyone had
even been aware that he had equal shares in the burgeoning
DIY company. By then his probity was beyond question and
the proprietor had waived his rule that the staff shouldn't be
involved in outside interests which might conceivably clash
with those of the paper.

'Have you heard any more about young Riley's death?'

She thought she detected an underlying tension in his
tone, a suggestion that his question stemmed from something more than casual curiosity, for George, like practically
everyone else, had had little time for Harry.

'Not a lot' she said. 'We haven't seen the pathologist's
report, but the police seem to think it was an accident.'

George nodded with a trace of satisfaction. 'I suppose he'd
been drinking. And then that cliff! Notoriously dangerous.
They should do something about it. Fence off the road. It's
only a few feet from the edge.'

'That's right, George, it is, isn't it?' It had been a long
time since she'd gone up to the cliff and she hadn't remembered how close the road was to it.

'Anyone . . .' she started to say, then stopped herself.
George Lacey seemed too curious. And it was only a thought.
Anyone could have driven Harry in whatever state to the
edge of the cliff and pushed him over. No one would see
them in the middle of the night and there would be no car
tracks to the spot.

'Anyone would be in danger, wouldn't they? Especially if
they'd been drinking,' she said quickly.

He studied her intently for a moment, but the next words

he uttered gave no hint that he might have caught her train of thought.

'Well, that'll be a nice, long-running story for the *Telegraph*.'

'The cliff danger or Harry's death?'

'The cliff, of course. I should think the other is open and shut. And I don't suppose there'll be many mourners in Seahaven. Nasty piece of work. Can't understand why Alec took him on in the first place.' It wasn't like George to speak so unfeelingly about anyone.

'Why . . . why did everyone have such a down on Harry?'

He looked at her, amused, as if hardly crediting her *naïveté*. 'You mean you didn't?'

'Not especially. He was brash, vulgar, pushy, but he was young, too, and keen and good at his job.'

'I'd say he had a darn sight too eager understanding of being good at your job. There are things . . .'

'What things, George?' she prodded him.

'Things best left alone.' He shook his head, then grinned down at her. 'Like your ham sandwich, it seems. Not hungry?'

'I'd forgotten it.'

'More interesting things to think about than ham sandwiches?'

'Maybe.' Suddenly, the sunny gardens seemed faintly malevolent and the pleasant George Lacey had shown a darker side of himself that Sheila hadn't suspected.

'Must get back.' She stood up hurriedly.

Then she paused and picked up the ham sandwich. She handed it to him. 'Here, it's yours.'

'No, thanks. I've eaten. I'll feed it to the birds.'

As she walked out of the gardens she could feel his eyes following her into the street.

When she got back to the office, Daphne Walters had abandoned her puce sweater and was devouring a jam doughnut along with the latest Jeffrey Archer paperback.

'Some man wanted you,' she said, without taking her eyes off the printed page.

'What man?'

'Rang twice.'

'Did he give a name or number?'

Daphne sighed, put down the paperback reluctantly and thumbed through a notebook in front of her.

'I put it down somewhere.'

'Well, for Christ's sake, *find* it, Daphne.'

The girl looked up at her with a pained expression. She was used to being bawled out by the others, but not by Sheila.

'Something go down the wrong way?' she sniffed.

'Daphne, please. I'm busy.'

'Don't think I'm not,' she grumbled, placing a plump arm strategically over the paperback. 'Here it is. Name of Slack. Funny name. It's a Brighton number. Do you want me to get it?'

Sheila nodded. Getting exasperated with Daphne, she'd found out long ago, was a waste of time. 'I'd really appreciate that,' she said, knowing full well that sarcasm was wasted on her.

'You just have to ask,' the girl called after her. 'Madam!'

Some day I'll have to speak to Alec about Daphne, Sheila thought, not for the first time.

'Oh, by the way.'

'What now, Daphne?' Sheila sighed.

'That chap Stride. You know. I told you Harry Riley was asking. My friend knew him. He was killed in a fire—with a couple of other boys. In an old warehouse, just outside Shoreham on the coast road. Big case, she said. I should have thought you'd have remembered.'

The name that had eluded her when Daphne first mentioned it clicked into place. It had happened two or three years before. The boys in their late teens, all with records of juvenile delinquency, had used the abandoned warehouse as a hide-out, probably for storing stolen goods although that was never proved. One night the ramshackle building, always a fire hazard, had burned down. The three inmates had perished in the flames. The police had acted smartly, arresting a man with a grudge against them. The evidence against him had been overwhelming and his conviction a foregone conclusion. He was now serving life imprisonment or twenty years with good behaviour.

But why would Harry have been interested in a case that had long since passed into history? And what was so special about the boy named Stride?

As she was digesting this fresh information, Sheila's call to Brighton was put through. Daphne could get a move on when it suited her. Sheila suspected she was listening in.

'Daphne, this is private,' she snapped at the telephone, more out of pique than any strong belief that Mr Slack had anything confidential to communicate. Probably just some irate reader with a bee in his bonnet.

The voice at the other end sounded hoarse and furtive, conjuring up a picture of a seedy little man with bad teeth in a dirty mac.

'Slack, here. Joe Slack,' it said, as if volunteering his name was betraying a trust.

'This is Sheila Tracy, Mr Slack. I'm returning your call.' There was a long silence.

'Sheila Tracy,' she repeated. 'The *Seahaven Telegraph*.'

'I heard,' the voice growled.

She was beginning to take an instant dislike to Mr Slack and was debating whether to put down the receiver when he came quickly to the point. 'I read that Harry Riley was dead. You see, we've got some unfinished business. You'd better come and see me.'

Sheila ignored the affrontery of the command, conscious of a rising excitement. At least the mysterious initials 'J.S.' in Harry's diary were now explained.

'I don't know how I could help you, Mr Slack,' she said

cautiously. 'Harry didn't confide much in anyone and I've no idea what business he could have had with you.'

'We'll get to that later. Let's just say I was doing some work for him. For the moment. He said if anything should happen to him I should get in touch with you. Said you were the only one he could trust. So that's what I'm doing. Getting in touch. Mind you, it's against my principles in my line of work.'

For a moment Sheila was speechless. She'd stopped listening after his extraordinary remark 'if anything should happen to him'. Certainly, Harry had had a strong sense of drama, but even he would hardly manufacture a threat to his life if none existed. And for someone who felt himself in danger, keeping a diary seemed a curiously risky undertaking. It was almost as if he had wanted Sheila to find it.

'Are you still there?'

'I . . . Mr Slack, what on earth would make Harry think he was in danger?'

'I told him he shouldn't meddle. Let sleeping dogs lie. He wouldn't listen. Said he had his reasons.'

'But why?' she said helplessly.

'Look, he said he trusted you but I don't trust telephones.' There was an unmistakable note of irritation in the unlovely voice. 'Too many ears listening in. Are you going to meet me or aren't you? If you won't, I'll forget it. I never wanted to be part of it, not when I realized what an eager beaver that little runt was.'

'Of course I'll meet you. But wouldn't it be best to go to the police?'

'What for? It was an accident, wasn't it? Have you got any proof that it wasn't?'

'No,' she admitted.

'Besides, the police and me . . . Well, I don't want to be messed up in it. I'm just doing right by him. Sort of last will and testament. Tomorrow morning. Say ten.'

'I'm not sure . . .' she started to say, then decided Joe
Slack was in no mood to accommodate the demands on her
time. 'All right. Ten. Tomorrow. What's your address?'

'No, not here. I've my clients,' he said importantly.
'There's a snack bar opposite the West Pier. You can't miss
it. Lucy's.'

'How will I know you?'

'Don't worry, I'll know you?'

The cloak and dagger deviousness of his arrangements
would have made her laugh in other circumstances. And
there would hardly be much of a risk meeting a strange man
in a snack bar in broad daylight. All the same, she'd like to
know a little more about her blind date.

'Mr Slack, I'll come, but you have to tell me first: who
are you?'

'Oh, you don't need to worry about me. I'm a private
investigator,' he said with an unsuitable touch of piety.
Pride in his calling, Sheila judged, was not a *trait* that came
naturally to Joe Slack.

CHAPTER 7

'Thank God, that's over,' breathed Sheila, settling herself
appreciatively in an alcove of the modest Italian restaurant
tucked in a side street away from the mainstream of Seahaven's limited night life.

'New?'

Stephen Gough nodded. 'Not long opened. The owner's
a friend of mine—from the old days. He used to be a waiter
at the Terrazza in Romilly Street. It's not lavish, but the
food's good.'

On cue, the owner—a gregarious Italian-Cockney who
answered to the name of Gino—bustled over with menus
and effusive greetings.

'Nice friends you have,' observed Sheila after they'd ordered.

'Which is more than I can say for yours.'

'They're no friends of mine. Well not really.'

As usual, he was putting her on the defensive, but in all conscience she couldn't blame him for his disapproval. The Festival committee meeting at the White Hart had started out as boringly as she'd anticipated, with Mrs Eleanor Rushton, to whom everyone deferred, firmly arbitrating in matters of trivial disagreement.

But as it proceeded Sheila had felt she detected an undercurrent of tension as if the committee were guarding some conspiratorial secret they feared might be revealed by an unwary word or gesture. The expected arguments were tinged with a hostility that, in the light of Harry Riley's death, now seemed to her to suggest a far more sinister motivation than the discussions actually warranted. Although on the surface the meeting went more or less according to accustomed plan.

While Seahaven enjoyed its annual Festival, the participants and spectators were creatures of ingrained habit who wouldn't take kindly to radical changes in format. But this time each proposal provoked snide or heated responses. They don't even like each other, thought Sheila. These nice, normal people with their smooth relationships don't like each other.

Ida Glaxton's pledge of a promenade entertainment from the Seahaven Musical Comedy Society and a sale of work and homemade produce from the Women's Institute was greeted with derision by Jack Murray. 'I suppose you'd prefer a nude show,' she sniffed, blushing.

John Agnew promised his Rotarians would organize parent-and-child races at the district sports centre. 'Weather permitting. Remember last year when it rained and only one father and son turned up for the three-legged race and we had to abandon it,' George Lacey grumbled.

'Well, if that's how you feel . . .'

'Please, gentlemen. I'm sure the weather will be kind' said Eleanor Rushton soothingly, but her voice had an unmistakable hint of warning in it.

The angry John Agnew got his revenge when George Lacey proposed that the local amateur soccer team, the Haverners, should be responsible for bring and buy stalls and outdoor bingo.

'That should draw the crowds. They're the laughing-stock of the amateur league. Haven't won a game in yonks,' laughed Agnew.

Edgar Blythe, as spokesman for the Council's policy and resources committee, proposed a lecture in the church hall on Sussex flora and fauna by an eminent but excruciatingly dull resident expert to lift the tone of the proceedings. He was voted down and subsided aggrieved, but he perked up when Lester Barnes suggested that all the local hotels should offer one Seahaven 'special' cocktail free for the period of the Festival to those who bought a raffle ticket and ordered another drink. Marion Blythe hoped that wouldn't lead to drunken orgies and the attraction of an unwelcome element of rowdies to the town. But, having sampled Lester Barnes's notion of a 'special' cocktail in the past (one part bitter lemon, one part orange juice, one part sweet white wine and a dash of angostura), Inspector Jimmy Grant thought that wouldn't be an insuperable problem for the police.

Jack Murray took it upon himself to organize the floats parading through the town centre (Ida Glaxton suggested musical comedy themes which, after some acrimonious discussion, was approved) and a beauty contest.

'But no bikinis,' Marion Blythe warned. 'You remember what happened last year.' (Last year in an unseasonal gale force wind one of the contestants had stumbled into the arms of an inebriated spectator who, hardly crediting his good luck, had untied her bikini top, exposing a goose-pimpled but ample bosom to full public view.) Periodically

Dr Bile raised doubts about the location of the St John Ambulance first aid unit.

While Sheila took notes, she had been uncomfortably aware of Stephen Gough's amused appraisal of this gathering of the Seahaven establishment in full flow. As he was a kind of local celebrity—if they hadn't read his books they'd certainly read the reviews—his presence at the meeting had been accepted with grudging agreement. 'Perhaps you might even make some useful comments on our plans,' Eleanor Rushton had said, thus setting the seal of her own valued approval on his role as observer. She had, he thought, the inherited knack of putting everyone at their ease and she was an uncommonly handsome woman who carried her years with ageless grace. She would also, he suspected, be an intimidating opponent.

Half way through the meeting Alec had arrived in his usual nonchalant manner, seemingly unconscious of the expectant pause in the conversation, as if the committee was waiting for him to impart some vital information which could hardly have much to do with running a town Festival, thought Sheila.

The moment of silent tension had passed as the cut-glass voice of Eleanor Rushton called the meeting to order.

The discussion had droned on for another half-hour, reaching an agreement which though inconclusive in detail was satisfactory in general.

'Then that's settled.' Eleanor Rushton was a decisive woman with a formidable regard for bureaucratic procedure. 'Perhaps Ida would be good enough to circulate an outline to all the members of the committee for submission to their individual sub-committees.' Ida Glaxton had volunteered to take notes of the meeting, an onerous task for which there were no other takers. 'And, of course, Miss Tracy will hold the report in the Press until the mayor has given it his sanction, although naturally there'll be no problem about that. He apologized for not being here, but pressing duties, you know.'

'And speaking of pressing duties, I'm afraid I'll have to leave now.' Inspector Jimmy Grant had sat through the meeting with good-humoured but increasing irritation. It was a waste of time he could have done without.

'Can't stop for a snifter, Jimmy?' To Jack Murray, stopping for a snifter seemed the right and proper reward for listening to a lot of old women promoting the archaic idea of Seahaven as a centre of riotous revelry. His conception of the town was as a lucrative area for property development, a dormitory offshoot of Brighton. Still, you had to keep sweet with the local powers-that-be. You never knew when you might need them.

'Sorry, Jack.' There was little love lost between the two men. Jack Murray had sailed too close to the wind too often in buying up desirable plots of land and then bending the building regulations of the Council to his own ends.

'Got your hands full with this Harry Riley business, I suppose.'

Sheila had wondered who would be the first to bring up the subject of Harry's death and she was surprised that it should be John Agnew. Harry had, after all, been assigned to cover the meeting for the paper and it was as if everyone had been carefully not mentioning him. He was a non-person. A fate which, had he been alive, would have caused Harry great chagrin.

Jimmy Grant had looked at John Agnew sceptically. 'He's not going to give much away' Stephen murmured in her ear.

'We're waiting for the post mortem tomorrow and we're pursuing our investigations.'

'You mean there are any investigations worth making?' Jack Murray sounded as if he'd already had a couple of snifters before the meeting. 'He must have been drunk, missed his footing and fell.'

'You don't expect me to discuss police matters here.'
Hiding his anger, Jimmy Grant got up to go.

But Murray wouldn't leave the subject alone. 'Damned
good thing, too. Little bleeder, poking around in matters
that don't—didn't—concern him.'

'Jack!' There was a warning note in George Lacey's voice.

'It's not the time . . .' Marion Blythe's high-pitched repri-
mand petered out as Jack Murray rounded on her.

'And don't you be so sanctimonious about the dead.
You'd have cheerfully cut his throat when he reported that
the God Almighty Wives' Guild had filched funds from their
charity works for the disabled to contribute to the National
Front. Substantially!'

'Mr Murray, that's _enough_!'

The peremptory tone of Eleanor Rushton's command
seemed to bring him to his senses. Christ, what had made
him go off the deep end like that! Riley! Bloody Riley!

'I'm sorry, ladies, sorry' he apologized. He mopped his
forehead and attempted, not very successfully, a boyish grin.
'I suppose he did get us all on the raw. But the poor boy's
dead, after all.'

As if to defuse an ugly situation there was a general
agreement that Harry Riley had been a nuisance to the
community but no one deserved to die such a tragic death.

Perhaps it was the sudden disgust she felt at their obvious
hypocrisy or merely an impulse she couldn't control that
caused Sheila to speak up for him.

'Harry wasn't so bad. He worked hard and he was a good
reporter. Maybe he went too far sometimes, but that's part
of a reporter's job.'

She looked round plaintively at Alec, pleading for a
reassuring word to back up her outburst. He shook his head,
smiling, as if to say, 'You're doing all right.'

'But we've never had any trouble with you, Miss Tracy,'
said Ida Glaxton.

No, thought Sheila, you never have. I've been meek and

accommodating and careful not to quote anything off the record, accepting what you tell me at face value, never questioning too hard. Perhaps now she knew what Stephen and her father and unlamented Harry had meant when they'd accused her of being too complacent.

Well, maybe it was time that she showed them she wasn't just sugar and spice and all things nice, charming Miss Tracy who could always be relied upon to present everything in the best possible light. Perhaps it was time that she, like Harry, took a risk.

'Anyway, if he were just a muck-raker, I doubt whether he'd have been so concerned about the fate of three boys who were burned to death in a fire long before he even joined the *Telegraph*,' she blurted out, embroidering Harry's interest in the Shoreham warehouse fire quite deliberately to suggest an altruistic motive which she doubted he had.

But the reaction it won her was unexpected and faintly alarming. There was no question but that they knew about the case of arson and murder to which she was referring. For what seemed an eternity they were silent, their eyes studying her intently, speculatively.

They had the effect of making her feel both stupid and vulnerable and she was aware that her nose was turning embarrassingly red, a nervous affliction when she was the centre of attention.

It was Alec who broke the silence. 'Of course, Sheila's right. Harry had his good points—even though most of you thought I was misguided to employ him.' His lightly dismissive remark, turned against himself, defused the tension, giving the committee an easy way out of the impasse Sheila had introduced. The social niceties asserted themselves.

She could hardly believe her ears as they fatuously shored up the gulf that had threatened to disrupt the meeting and sour the relationships of the committee members. Together they gratefully re-established a solid front.

'The young, after all, do tend to be headstrong . . .'

'And the poor boy must have had an unfortunate background . . .' This was pure assumption. Harry's background was a secret he kept to himself.

'Alec should be congratulated on giving a bright youngster a chance . . .'

'It's just so tragic . . .'

'Tragic . . .'

'Really, Edgar, the council should do something about that cliff . . .'

It was on this note of mutual sympathy for a dead young man whose faults were probably due to an underprivileged upbringing that the meeting broke up.

The members studiously ignored Sheila, who blew her nose, closed her notebook and shrugged off Stephen's gentle attempt to soothe her feelings.

'You enjoyed that, didn't you?' she snapped at Alec. 'Watching me squirm, watching them sniping at each other over Harry!'

'It relieved the monotony.'

'Bastard!'

'That's no way to speak to your editor, Sheila!' He put his arm around her. 'You mustn't take it all so *seriously*. It's just Seahaven.'

'Dead *is* serious.'

Alec sighed. 'Steve, take her away, feed her and make her happy.'

The two men exchanged wry smiles over her head.

Infuriated, she turned on the pair of them. 'And I won't be treated like some feather-brained little ninny, just to boost your insufferable male egos. If this is Seahaven you can—you can feed it to the fish.'

She was so unused to losing her temper that the moment of anger collapsed in a fit of laughter. Feeding Seahaven to the fish! She couldn't even conjure up a worthwhile insult.

By the time they'd strolled to Gino's restaurant she'd

recovered her habitual good humour. The excellent *gnocchi alla Romana* and *osso buco* lubricated with several glasses of *soave* helped too.

As she sipped her *cappuccino* she studied her companion who was thumbing through the pages of Harry's diary and decided he looked uncommonly like her father as a younger man: strong-boned and powerfully built, but with the same fastidious mind that seemed so out of key with his appearance. Maybe that's why she was attracted to him, maybe she was searching for another father image. Although even as the thought struck her she knew it to be untrue. Whatever he wasn't, Stephen Gough was his own man.

'Steve, do you think I made a fool of myself?'

He didn't take his eyes from the diary. 'No. But I think you may have made a target of yourself.'

'What do you mean—target?'

He looked up finally and took her hand. He answered her question with another surprising one.

'What did you feel about that meeting, those people?'

She considered his query for a moment, realizing that he meant it seriously. 'I felt they, some of them, had something to hide, that they disliked Harry because he was too astute for them. I felt they were a bunch of hypocrites who, when challenged, could behave like yah-boo schoolboys in the playground.'

'And that's all?'

'Steve, I've known these people practically all my life. Certainly since I've been working for the *Telegraph*. I agree they showed a side I hadn't seen before. But what else is there?'

'Evil.'

She stared at him, disbelievingly. 'What? *Evil*! You have to be joking. You should stick to science fiction.'

'I'm not joking and you know I'm not. When you brought up the subject of the fire in the warehouse, more than one person in that room could have cheerfully killed you. Harry may be dead, but, for your own sake, Sheila, you must face the fact that now it's you who is in the firing line.'

CHAPTER 8

'Why are you trying to frighten me, Steve?' She withdrew her hand from his abruptly and looked pointedly at her watch.

'No, please, don't cut off, Sheila. Listen to me. If I'd known how deep this thing was I wouldn't have let you stumble into it so—' he searched for a word that wouldn't alarm her further—'so incautiously. I should have told you to forget it. I'd underestimated how stubborn you were underneath that docile exterior. Maybe you've a more powerful sense of justice than all of us. It's admirable. But I've seen too many admirable and righteous people ground down by . . .'

' . . . the forces of evil?' Her attempt at a facetious riposte failed dismally.

'Exactly.' He smiled reassuringly. 'Well, the damage is done. They know you know—something. But they don't know what and you're not going to make any silly mistakes like that again. Not while I'm around.'

Even the solemnity of his warning couldn't diminish the glow of pleasure his words generated in her.

'You sound very protective,' she said, hoping it didn't come out as unduly coquettish. If there was anything she loathed in her sex it was the simpering of a calculated flirt.

'If ever a lady was in need of care and protection, it's you,' he replied fondly. Then in a brusque down-to-business manner he added, 'Besides, you're reviving my old investigative instincts. Might be fun finding out what old—young —Harry had up his sleeve.' He noticed her frown at the word 'fun'. 'I didn't mean fun. I just think perhaps you, I, we, owe it to Harry.'

He picked up the diary. 'Now *this* is lethal.'

'Lethal! I couldn't make any sense out of it, except for that note about "Es" and "Mart" and that didn't make much sense either.'

'Don't you believe it. For a secretive reporter he was a damned sight too lax in keeping any sort of diary. You'd better let me hang on to it. If I thought it would be of any use to the police I'd hand it over. Jimmy Grant is a good sort. Straight. But I doubt whether they'd have the time or the inclination to even try to decode it. If the inquest doesn't come up with any spectacular new findings it's more than likely that the verdict will be misadventure. No question, I imagine, of suicide.'

Sheila found herself catching his mood of excitement. 'At least we've found out who J.S. is. Joe Slack.' She'd filled him in over their meal about her conversation and proposed meeting with the private investigator in Brighton, as well as Harry's interest in the boy named Stride, one of the victims of the warehouse fire.

'That's another thing. I'm not sure you should see him alone. He sounds like some cheap con man who fancies himself as a private eye.'

'What possible harm could come to me in a Brighton snack bar in the middle of the day?'

He conceded that. 'But play it very cool. Act as if you're simply meeting him because Harry was a colleague and that's what he wanted. Let him do the talking. And, for God's sake, don't part with any money. Get in touch with me as soon as you've seen him.'

'You're really getting steamed up about this.' He'd always seemed so aloof, so uninvolved, before.

He brushed aside her observation as irrelevant. 'I can do a little digging around myself. Remember, I'm a member of the bridge group that meets on Wednesdays. Not that I go very often. But George, Alec, Jack Murray, Edgar and Jimmy Grant all play bridge there and it's surprising what people let slip when they draw the dummy hand. I'd like to know a bit more about Murray's business dealings and Marion Blythe's Wives' Guild. Could be nothing. Could be everything. And, incidentally, why would Alec turn up tonight? You were doing the reporting.'

'Oh, I don't know. He's unpredictable. Likes to keep tabs on what's going on. If he feels like it or thinks it's important to the paper he occasionally sits in on meetings and interviews. He's not as unflappable as he seems.'

'Strange he should have championed Harry against all that opposition.'

It was a thought that had struck her more than once and she'd always arrived at the same conclusion. 'I believe he really admired Harry's guts. He was genuinely convinced that he'd be an asset to the paper, shake it out of its sloth, if you like. I know he appears a sort of dilettante editor and the *Seahaven Telegraph* is hardly *The Times*. But deep down he cares about it. He wants to make it bright and lively and not just a propaganda hand-out for the town. It's been an uphill battle for him.'

'If he cares that much about good journalism it's a wonder he stayed here.'

Sheila smiled. He was such an outsider. 'You still don't understand Seahaven, do you, Steve? It's a nice bachelor life. The paper isn't the be-all and end-all of everything to him. He's got his business with George. A comfortable home. A lot of outside interests. A standing in the community. It counts for a good deal.'

Stephen shook his head. In the cut-throat world of true, professional newspapermen journalism *was* their life. It consumed every waking hour, destroyed relationships, broke up marriages and homes and, quite often, ruined your health. It was a demon that wouldn't let go unless, like Fred Happer, you saw the light and even then that demon pursued him to peaceful Seahaven. Maybe, thought Steve, it's even pursuing *me*, now.

'Bullseye' he mused. 'That's another point. What did Harry find that was such a bullseye? Much about the time Fred found him combing the files, you say.'

'I wouldn't know where to begin. The files are stored after a year. It could have been any edition from 1984 to when the paper was launched after the First World War. Maybe it was something to do with the reports on the Shoreham fire and the trial. I can easily look them up.'

'No, you can't. Not yet. You blew that one this evening. It would be better to let that little contretemps die down before you start digging through the back copies of the paper. I don't imagine much happens at your office that goes unobserved.'

Remembering the furtive secrecy she'd employed in uncovering Harry's diary, Sheila had to admit that privacy was in short supply at the *Seahaven Telegraph*.

They suddenly realized it was nearing midnight. Behind the bar, Gino was whistling tunelessly through his teeth, not wanting to disturb his customers but just to remind them that the hour was late and they were the only diners left in the place.

'I think,' said Sheila, feeling acutely embarrassed, 'he's trying to tell us something.'

Stephen didn't seem to hear her. He was still poring over the contents of the diary. 'Wait! This last entry of Harry's. "Palace cinema. 8.0 pm."'

'Look, Steve, we're keeping the man about. He wants to shut up.'

'So let him hang about a few minutes longer. Gino won't mind.'

'It's perfectly plain,' she said, not bothering to disguise her exasperation. 'It's about the only simple fact in the damned diary. Harry went to the Palace the evening he died. The police know that. He was seen in the back row, watching some porny movie called *Punk Lust*. The usherette identified him. What's so special about that? I admit Harry didn't strike me as the kind who'd waste his time on that sort of trash. But there's no accounting for tastes.'

'You're missing the point. If you were going to the cinema on your own would you bother to make a note of it, unless you were one of those amateur critics who wrote potted reviews of every film or play you saw? And Harry wasn't.'

'So. It was out of character . . .'

'Oh no it wasn't. 8.0 pm. Harry wasn't going to the cinema to enjoy a little vicarious sex and violence. He was meeting someone there. At 8.0 pm. And that meeting was important enough—and perhaps unexpected enough—for him to jot it down. In some haste, I'd say, judging by his scrawl.'

Gino's whistling was now accompanied by a determined tapping of his fingers on the counter, but, for once, Sheila forgot her embarrassment, ignoring the insistent suggestion that they should pay the bill and leave.

'It could have been Molly Arkwright . . . no, she said he was supposed to be meeting her at the disco later. Then who . . . ?'

'If we knew that we wouldn't be sitting here trying to fathom why Harry died.'

He signalled to Gino, who rushed over with alacrity and presented the bill. 'I hope you enjoyed your meal, Mr Gough. Nice to see you again.'

'First rate, Gino. Sorry we kept you so late.'

Gino beamed. Now that they were actually going he could afford to be indulgent. 'I understand,' he asserted conspiratorially.

Good God, he thinks we're lovers. Sheila suppressed an impulse to giggle.

'I'm sure you do, Gino. Maybe Miss Tracy will write up the restaurant in her column.'

Gino beamed appreciatively, more at the large tip Stephen left behind than at the prospect of a write-up in the *Seahaven Telegraph*.

They drove back in silence to Sheila's home which was shrouded in darkness. Andrew had obviously gone to bed.

Depositing her on her doorstep, Stephen kissed her lightly on the lips. It was an agreeable sensation. In the time they'd known each other he'd never displayed any physical sign of affection.

'What's that for?'

'I'm not sure. Moral support.' He traced his forefinger down her cheek and round her jawline. 'Your nose is red.'

'Damn!'

'Sheila, I'm not kidding. Be careful.' He studied her seriously for a few moments then turned on his heel and strode down the drive to his car.

As she switched on the light in the hall a flimsy sheet of paper which had been lodged in the letter-box fluttered to the floor. Idly she picked it up, her mind a jumble of impressions—about Steve, Harry, the fraught committee meeting and something else, less tangible, an underlying sense of disquiet. It was as if tonight she had declared herself boldly and, perhaps, recklessly. She would never be the same nice, quiet, predictable Sheila again. People her instincts and upbringing had taught her to respect had shown themselves to be petty at best or worse than devious.

She cast her eyes over the slip of paper in her hand. It was a standard circular for a jumble sale, the kind that was distributed to every house in the town. She was about to drop it on the hall table, with a mental reminder to look out some suitable jumble, when she noticed a curt message written in capital letters on the back. The three words sent a shiver up her spine.

'Forget Harry Riley.'

CHAPTER 9

Joe Slack had told Sheila that she couldn't miss Lucy's and he'd been right. Long before she spotted the poky snack bar within nodding distance of the West Pier at Brighton, the rank odour of soggy chips-with-everything assailed her nostrils. It was too early for day trippers, but some workmen from a nearby building site were tucking into mounds of sausage, eggs and the inevitable chips washed down with tea from a giant urn on the counter. They looked up as she came in and made cheeky faces at each other. 'Lost your way, sweetheart?' one said between mouthfuls. The others grinned. But when she didn't reply they ignored her.

Apart from a surly woman with a flushed face in a none too clean apron behind the counter, there seemed to be no one else in the snack bar. 'What can I get you?' the woman demanded, idly wiping a damp cloth over the formica top.

Sheila looked doubtfully at the dishwater tea. 'Coffee. Black.' Not taking her eyes off Sheila, as if she half expected her to pocket the spoons, the woman scooped a meagre measure of instant into a mug and slopped hot water on top of it. 'Sugar on the tables.' She indicated a row of small benches and stools lined up in martial formation by the low side windows which afforded a view on to the building site.

'Looking for someone?' The woman's curiosity got the better of her suspicion. However inconspicuous Sheila tried to make herself, she was obviously not the kind of customer Lucy's usually attracted.

'Just . . . just meeting a friend,' Sheila replied falteringly. She supposed Joe Slack was a regular. On the other hand, he might have picked the snack bar because it was off the track of his usual haunts.

The woman sniffed and with a sergeant-major bellow called through the hatch to the kitchen.

'Bert! Have you fixed that fryer yet?'

'It's coming,' a weary voice assured her.

'Well, hurry it up.'

One of the workmen held up a pale, flabby chip in a grimy thumb and forefinger. 'We ought to get a rebate, Lucy.'

'That'll be the day,' Lucy barked. 'Can I help it if the fryer's on the blink?'

Sheila sipped her coffee and wished she hadn't given up smoking. The memory of that printed warning 'Forget Harry Riley' the night before kept triggering off alarm bells in her mind. She looked at her watch. It was five past ten. Either punctuality wasn't one of Joe Slack's virtues or he was biding his time, letting her sweat out the waiting period until he deemed it fit to put in an appearance.

I'll give him ten minutes, she thought, studiously avoiding the attention of the workmen who, now replete, were lighting up cigarettes and draining the dregs of their tea. She affected a consuming interest in the building site across the way. As the men lumbered to the counter and paid their bills, trading good-natured insults with Lucy about the quality of the food, she spotted a wiry little figure threading his way through the debris of the site towards the snack bar. Although the skies were cloudless and the temperature was rising into the high sixties Fahrenheit, he was wearing a grey belted raincoat which, together with his quick, darting movements, made him look like an anxious field mouse dodging the pursuit of a predator.

Then he slid out of her vision, round the corner. As the workmen poured out of the door back to the job, she saw him standing almost courteously aside to let them through. He had the air of a man who was accustomed to subsiding into the woodwork. She doubted whether any of the men noticed him or, if they did, they'd forget him instantly.

Another moment or two passed before he entered the snack bar.

He nodded at Lucy, who raised her bushy, unplucked eyebrows. 'Well, well!' she smirked, glancing at Sheila. 'The usual?'

He nodded again and, without introducing himself or even acknowledging her presence, sat awkwardly on the stool across the table from Sheila.

Lucy plonked a mug of tea in front of him, slopping a third of it on the table. 'Chelsea bun, toasted,' he said in the same hoarse voice Sheila had heard over the telephone.

'Sorry. Toaster's packed up. Bert's working on it.' Bert, it seemed, was having a busy morning.

'All right. Plain.'

It wasn't until he'd munched his way with his rabbitty teeth through half the bun that he paid any attention to Sheila.

'Not quite your style, I expect. But there's not much doing here this time of day and we can talk, private like.'

'You were late,' she said acidly.

He ignored the rebuke. 'Have to be careful in my line of business.'

As he finished the Chelsea bun and licked his fingers she decided Stephen's assessment of Joe Slack probably wasn't far wrong. Despite the decently cut raincoat, there was a seedy furtiveness about him, his beady eyes in a thin, lined face never met hers, but they seemed to be taking in everything from the clotted sugar on the spoon in the sugar bowl to the unconcerned glances of occasional passers-by as they looked in the window. His wispy grey hair had probably been flattened neatly across his scalp that morning but the wind off the shore had rearranged it, separating the strands and giving them the appearance of an unholy halo round his head.

'Harry held you in high regard,' he said. 'Poor little sod!'

Joe Slack was obviously a man who took his time before getting to the point. All the same, Sheila had had about enough of his delaying tactics and the smell of rancid fat from the kitchen was beginning to make her feel nauseous.

'Look, Mr Slack, I haven't got all day . . .'

'Hold you horses! You know why you're here and I know why you're here. I've got something to tell and you want to hear it. Right?'

She nodded. 'Just what kind of association did Harry have with you?' It was as good a place to start as anywhere.

'I helped him,' he said slyly. 'Gave him bits of information when he couldn't get it for himself. Remember the piece he did on that cricket club fiddle? That was me—well, mostly. I'm good at that.'

I'll just bet you are, she thought. 'Why did Harry think something might happen to him?'

He assumed an air of injured innocence. 'Haven't a clue. I didn't ask questions. I got the stuff . . .'

'Stuff?'

'Information,' he explained, irritated at her obtuseness. 'And he paid up. He still owes me a bundle of money,' he added ruefully.

And I bet he'd already paid you a bundle, thought Sheila.

When she didn't rise to the bait with an offer to replenish his resources, he picked his teeth and sighed. 'Oh well, water under the bridge, I suppose. Can't get money out of a corpse, can you?'

Even he had the grace to assume a placating sympathy when he saw her reaction to his crass remark. 'I mean, old Harry would see the joke. He wasn't sentimental, Harry. Just, well, passionate, I suppose you could say.'

'Passionate about what?' she said quickly. Passion wasn't an emotion she'd have associated with Harry.

His little eyes gleamed with pleasure, realizing he'd caught her off guard.

With infuriating preciseness he took out a bag of tobacco and cigarette papers and rolled himself a cigarette.

Before lighting the frayed ends of tobacco he smiled at

her greedily. 'Caught you, didn't I? His cousin. He was passionate about his cousin. Martin Bailey.'

'Bailey!' The name, like that of Stride when Daphne had mentioned him, had a nagging but unidentifiable familiarity. Certainly he had to be the 'Mart' in Harry's diary.

'That's right, Bailey.' He seemed to be cogitating on the mileage and possible rewards he might get out of this evidence of Harry's past which she obviously hadn't known, then apparently decided both were negligible. It was all, after all, on the record.

'He was the bloke who got life after that warehouse fire Shoreham way—three years ago or thereabouts. Three kids, well, more than kids, layabouts the lot of them, died in it.'

'And Bailey was Harry's cousin!'

'Kept it quiet, did he? Well, in a nice place like Seahaven, I don't suppose he'd wanted it known that his cousin was a convicted murderer.' The 'nice place like Seahaven' came out more as a term of ridicule than as a compliment.

'Even so, why would Harry engage you to dig out the facts of the case? He must have lived through it and he could check it up in the newspaper records and trial transcripts if he wanted to.'

His expression was smugly mocking, making Sheila feel uncomfortably thick-witted.

'Oh, don't you worry, Harry knew all the facts. The facts that sent Bailey down. He, Bailey, was known to have had a flaming row, very public, with the boys. They were drug-pushers, you know. And he was spotted in the district on the night, buying a can of petrol. Then a few minutes before the blaze, a neighbour had seen him near the warehouse.

'The police had an open and shut case,' Slack went on. 'Bailey couldn't account for anything. Leastways, not to the judge or the jury's satisfaction. Prosecution made a meal of him and the defence counsel did a sloppy job. The general feeling was that it was a settling of scores between scum.'

As he spoke, the vague details of the case came back to Sheila. It hadn't caused much of a stir in Seahaven, which tended to keep aloof from the crime and swift punishment that was a feature of life among what it regarded as the lawless underworld along the coast. Because that sort of thing didn't happen in Seahaven it didn't concern the town.

'But Harry didn't buy that? He thought Martin Bailey was innocent?' She was beginning to catch on to Harry's train of thought.

Slack nodded approvingly. Maybe she wasn't as dim and prissy as she'd seemed at first.

'He was *convinced* he was innocent. Mind you, it could just have been family feeling, Bailey being his only living relative. Bailey had a record, although he swore at the trial he was clean. Said since he'd married, his wife had kept him on the straight and narrow. There was a baby, I believe.'

'Es!'

'Es?'

'His wife.'

Slack frowned, thinking back. 'Edith. Ethel. Esther. Something like that.'

'Esther. Has to be.'

'How do you know her name, then?' Slack said suspiciously.

That's for you to find out, thought Sheila. 'Oh, he mentioned it once. Do you happen to know if she's alive, where she lives?'

'What's in it for me?'

'Come on, Mr Slack. All I've got to do is look it up in the electoral register or go to the police.'

At her mention of the police his sallow complexion took on an even more bilious hue.

'That's the trouble with you reporters, you know too much,' he grumbled. 'Most of my clients wouldn't think of that. Times are hard. Even the divorce market isn't what it used to be.'

'Mr Slack, you still haven't told me what Harry was

paying you for, regarding the Bailey case.' Joe Slack's hard times were his concern, not hers.

He looked aggrieved. No feelings, these modern women. 'You're a hard lady,' he said, then: 'Hadley Avenue, one of those little streets off the harbour. Can't remember the number. But I expect she's known. Bailey's wife.'

Sheila made a mental note of the address. 'Right. Now what else?' She was getting the measure of Joe Slack. If you let him, he'd go on whining forever. But he was very receptive to a short, sharp retort.

'Like I said, Harry was sure Bailey was innocent.'

'A frame-up?'

He pursed his thin lips, licking off a shred of tobacco. 'Ooh, I wouldn't say anything as definite as that. More like negligence. His barrister—legal aid—wasn't exactly a ball of fire. And the police were satisfied.'

'And Harry thought there was a lot more to uncover even after Bailey's conviction?' she prodded him.

'He asked me to find out all I could about the boys who were killed in the fire.'

'Why would he do that?'

'How should I know? I just did what I was paid for. It wasn't easy, either. Very close-mouthed, all the relatives and mates. I had to sweeten them up. Cost, you know.' Money weighed heavily with Joe Slack.

'But you did come up with some information in the end?'

'Naturally. Joe Slack never gives in. I've my reputation in the business to think about. All the kids had some kind of form, juvenile stuff mostly at first—nicking hub caps, joyriding, being a public nuisance. Stuff like that. Then they were into drugs, pushing a little on the side.'

'But was there anyone else who could have wanted to kill them?'

'Maybe. In their game. But there are easier ways of settling scores and no one the wiser. It looked more like retribution to me.'

It was a strange, Biblical term for Joe Slack to use.

'What was Harry's reaction when you told him this?'

'Funny, he sort of discounted it, you know. Until I told him about Stride. Billy Stride. He was one of the boys. No more than sixteen. He'd been had up for rape. She'd only been fourteen and not one of those girls who ask for it. Nicely brought up. Just dead unlucky. Stride was lucky, though. Apparently, he was a charmer, could put on the injured act when it suited him. Deprived childhood, bad environment. His social worker believed him and put up a good case for him. The magistrate must have been asleep at the hearing. He got off with probation after the psychiatrist's report. He was under age anyway. And the social worker convinced them—God knows how!—that sending him away to a place for young offenders would be—how do you say? —counter-productive. Amazing what you can get away with if you use the right words!'

'And that's what interested Harry!' A scenario was beginning to write itself in Sheila's head, fortified by long-buried recollections that were now re-emerging in the light of Joe Slack's story. 'You don't happen to know the name of the girl who was raped?'

His reply didn't altogether surprise her.

'Someone up your way. Rushton. That's right. Sarah Rushton. Not that her name or Stride's got into the papers, both of them being minors. Know her?'

'No. But I know her mother.'

CHAPTER 10

'Intriguing!' said Stephen Gough.

'It's more than intriguing. You must admit it puts a whole new complexion on Harry's death.'

Under the eyes of Queen Victoria, whose formidable

statue guarded the entrance to Hove's Grand Avenue, they were walking along the promenade which edges the coastline from Brighton to Shoreham.

Stephen had insisted on meeting Sheila after she'd kept her appointment with Joe Slack, despite her protestations over the phone that she was perfectly well able to look after herself. He had seemed more perturbed about the note she'd received the previous night than she was herself.

'Did you believe him?'

'Slack? I think so. Why would he lie? After all, he got in touch with me in the first place because Harry told him to.'

'You've only his word for that. Maybe whoever wrote that warning to you put him up to it earlier. And, incidentally, I still think it's worth taking to the police. Or just let me give it to Jimmy Grant. I doubt whether there's much he can do about it. Ordinary circular. Printed capitals. But at least he'd be aware of it.'

She agreed that made sense, even though the more she delved into Harry's secrets the less confidence she felt in those members of the Seahaven establishment who had hitherto appeared to her so upstanding and respectable. Everyone, everything, she'd trusted before seemed suspect, making her feel both vulnerable and angry.

Stephen sensed her reluctance. 'Look, Sheila, somewhere at the root of this mess may be one or possibly two supposedly upright citizens who had enough to hide to murder for it. That's just a supposition, but let's take it as fact. But even if it were fact, that doesn't mean an entire community is to blame or is involved. It's not a conspiracy, for Heaven's sake.'

'But you're the one who keeps telling me to take that note seriously, to be careful. "You're in the firing line." Your very words,' she rounded on him testily.

He stopped, turned her towards him and placed his hands firmly on her shoulders. 'Sheila, I'm not underestimating the danger you might be in. I just don't want you *over-*

reacting. What makes you think you'd be any better at uncovering the truth than the police?'

'Because I bloody *care*!'

'And they don't? That's sheer hysteria.'

'You've changed your tune since last night.'

'That was last night. Before you received that note. I've been thinking a lot since you told me about it.'

She searched his face for an answer to a question that was forming in her mind and found it. 'You've done more than that, haven't you? You've been in touch with Jimmy Grant.'

She felt his hands relax on her shoulders. 'Yes.'

'And what did he say?'

'That he'd look into it. But he couldn't do anything without your cooperation.'

'Oh, give him the damned thing.' She rummaged through her shoulder-bag and produced the crumpled circular. 'Much good it will do him—or me. If the police can send Martin Bailey to gaol for a crime he didn't commit. . . .'

'The police didn't. The jury and judge did. And there you go, over-reacting again. Just because Harry thought his cousin was innocent doesn't *make* him innocent. Sheila, you know who you remind me of? No don't turn away. Listen. When I was covering the war in Viet Nam, one of the jingoistic tabloids sent out a very green, but bright and opinionated journalist to report on it. He came with all kinds of preconceived ideas about the righteousness of the American involvement out there and the villainy of the North Vietnamese. He'd never seen war at first hand and knew very little about the political background to it or the history of Indo-China.'

'What the hell has this to do with Harry and Martin Bailey and Billy Stride—or me, come to that?'

Stephen ignored her interruption. 'It was a shattering experience for every reporter who was out there. But it was worse for him. When he saw the death and destruction, the torment suffered by the civilian population, the wasting of whole villages, he changed his attitude completely. He immediately assumed that everything the Americans and the West did was venal and corrupt. He ignored the atrocities and intimidation on the other side. The Communists suddenly were a hundred per cent right. He had switched heroes as readily as he'd accepted the American version of the facts in the first place. He resigned from the paper and now he's a Marxist activist for the militant left wing of the Labour Party. He's just as blinkered now as he was before.'

The pain it obviously caused him to recall that traumatic episode in a career he seldom spoke about was etched on his face.

'It's a pretty extreme analogy,' she said softly. 'But I see your point.'

'All your life, Sheila, you've believed the best of the town, the people you've grown up with. You've never questioned it or them. Now, suddenly, because of Harry, you're seeing them in a different light. So, everything about them is bad. I know how you feel. In your small way you're going through what that reporter went through. It's not easy to strike a balance, keep things in perspective. But until you do you won't solve anything and afterwards you'll just be left hating people for doing no more harm than just being human, warts and all.'

'And what about those forces of evil you spoke of so eloquently last night?'

He grinned. 'Maybe *I* was over-reacting. There are forces of good too. Just remember. Softly, softly, catchee monkey! Come on, let's find a pub.' He took her arm brusquely and hurried her to the nearest watering hole.

When they were seated in a quiet alcove of the cosy pub sipping their gins and tonic, she felt a warm glow that wasn't entirely due to the welcome intake of alcohol. She knew what it had cost him to relive past memories he'd buried in his new leisurely life in Seahaven and his science fiction novels.

'That was quite a lecture. Why?'

He fingered his glass thoughtfully. 'I kept running over the conversation we had at Gino's last night while I was waiting for you in the car, knowing you were seeing that man Slack and wondering what you were letting yourself in for. I admit I was at fault for egging you on. I just don't want you to blunder foolhardily into something that may be bigger than you or I could handle. I figured the only way to make you aware of what you're taking on, really aware, was to scare you a little.'

'You succeeded. But I'm not giving up.'

'I wouldn't expect you to. That's one of the reasons why I think I love you.'

She wished she could control the flush that, unbidden, was burning her cheeks and turning her nose that unseemly red.

'What am I supposed to say to that?'

'Nothing—yet. I'm a cautious man.'

'I'm a cautious woman.'

'Remember you said that—and not just in the way we're trying not to talk about right now.' He gripped her hand, then let it go just as abruptly. 'OK. Back to Joe Slack.'

'I thought you'd never get around to him again.'

'I wish to God we didn't have to. He sounds what in polite company might be described as an unsavoury character. But he did come up with a couple of leads. You say you knew about Stride and this rape charge?'

Mention of Billy Stride brought her sharply down to earth.

'I knew about the rape, but not that Stride was the boy who committed it. At least I didn't take it in at the time. The only vague connection his name made in my mind was as one of the victims of the fire. Like Slack said, both he and the girl were minors, so their names weren't reported. I'm not sure we even reported it at all in the *Telegraph*—or, if we did, it was just a fairly noncommittal paragraph.'

'Why was that?'

'Out of deference to Eleanor Rushton's feelings—and her daughter's.'

'Whose decision was that? Alec's?'

'No, not especially. Just in general. We all felt on the paper—Fred Happer particularly—that it was the decent thing to do. It was hardly headline news, after all. Rape is ugly, but it's not all that uncommon—even in Seahaven. And it happened several years ago. A lot's happened since then.'

'Can you recall any of the details?'

She shook her head. 'Not many. I believe the girl Sarah had gone to a party in Brighton with her brother, Nicholas. He's quite a bit older than her—four years or so. She'd left before him, was making her way to a taxi-rank in Brighton and it happened. That's all I know. I assume the police picked up Stride and she identified him.'

'A fourteen-year-old girl walking the streets of Brighton at night. Doesn't sound very sensible. Where was her brother?'

'Still at the party, I suppose. Nicholas, I gather, is something of a thorn in the side of Eleanor Rushton's flesh. Bit of a layabout, no real job, but then he doesn't need to work. She's loaded. Her husband left her very well provided. She hardly ever talks about him, Nicholas. She certainly wouldn't to me. I really don't know her very well at all. Just professionally, interviews, occasionally I get invited to her charity teas. She's terribly upper-crust Seahaven.'

'And the daughter?'

'Last I heard, she was abroad. But that was ages ago. She's never around.'

'Well, it's worth looking into. Maybe Jimmy Grant . . .'

'No, Dad,' she came in quickly. Although she'd accepted Stephen's arguments meekly enough, whether from cussedness or conviction, she still refused to surrender totally her own independent line of inquiry 'I'll ask Dad. He had a lot of business dealings with Eleanor Rushton. Besides—he won't lecture me.'

'Don't you be too sure. Andrew and I are like minds,' he reminded her. Which was true. 'Anyway, now we're here we might as well make use of the time. I think I'll go to the pictures. I rather fancy seeing *Punk Lust*. They're bound to have an early screening.'

She almost choked over the sliver of gin-soaked lemon peel she was chewing. 'I thought you were more the Ingmar Bergman and Woody Allen type. *Punk Lust* doesn't seem your style.'

'No, but the usherette at the Palace may be.' He patted her on the back. 'Choke up! She might even be able to shed some light on Harry's date that night in the cinema.'

'And I'm not invited?'

'Not this time. If two people start asking questions her memory might freeze.'

'All right, if you're going to be gainfully employed, I shall be too. Hadley Avenue can't be far from here. I'll go and find Esther Bailey.' Anticipating his disapproval, she added smartly, 'I promise. Caution! But I'm on her—and Harry's —side. She won't see me as a threat.'

'Well, I don't like it, but . . . Want some advice?'

'Try me,' she said guardedly.

'You're a friend of Harry's. You know they were related by marriage. You just want to offer your condolences. Don't launch into the Bailey case straight away. She'll probably come around to it anyway.'

She smiled at him, too sweetly. 'You really don't rate me very highly as a reporter, do you? I know the rules as well as you do. Soften them up first and then you'll get the nitty gritty. Steve, just when you're being nice you start being infuriating. I'm not a child.'

As he levered his towering frame out of the tiny alcove,

he looked down at her as if seeing her seriously and objectively for the first time. 'No, you're not, are you!'

She allowed herself the luxury of allowing his eyes to play on her face for a few more moments. 'I suppose we should go,' she said finally.

'I suppose we should.'

The pub was filling up with regulars as they made their way through the swinging saloon bar door and parted.

When she found it after making a few inquiries from passers-by and taking two wrong turns, Hadley Avenue turned out to be one of a maze of run-down little streets of once-neat workmen's cottages which funnelled off the broad sweep of Shoreham Harbour. If it had once seemed relatively prosperous there were no signs of it now. Time, weather and the fluctuations of the harbour's fortunes had combined to give it a demoralized air.

The houses fronted straight on to the pavement where a few sad-looking birch trees might once have justified its claim to be an avenue. They were simple two-up, two-down residences, the paint peeling forlornly off the woodwork as if their owners had long since given up the challenge of keeping them in a decent state of repair. A few had printed notices in the windows, 'Bed and Breakfast,' with little hope of attracting customers. Occasionally long-haul lorry-drivers, bringing goods to the harbour, stayed overnight, but less and less as the motorways opened up the fast routes between the ports and the cities.

She asked a bunch of children kicking a football around the parked cars, which looked as if they'd taken root there, if they knew where Mrs Bailey lived.

They surveyed her sceptically, continuing their game until one scored a direct hit on the bonnet of an elderly Ford.

'Own goal,' his pal yelled.

'Gertcha,' the scorer replied. As they started to scuffle,

Sheila turned away and had decided to knock on the first door when the boy called after her.

'What's it worth?' he said, wiping away a dewdrop from his dripping nose with a grimy forefinger.

'Five p,' she offered.

'Make it ten.'

'Ten.'

'Last house up there.'

'Right or left?'

He considered, then gave up. 'There,' he said, pointing with his right hand.

She fished a ten-pence piece out of her purse. 'Thanks.'

He pocketed it swiftly. 'Miserable cow!' As she walked down the street she wasn't sure whether he was referring to her or Esther Bailey.

CHAPTER 11

The house at the far end of the street was sprucer than its neighbours. There were small, caring touches that set it apart from the others whose owners appeared to have given up the losing battle against dirt, pollution and indolence. The paintwork and metal fixtures on the front door were gleaming. There were crisp, chintz curtains at the windows and a pocket of garden at the side had been lovingly tended. Whatever else Esther Bailey might be, she was obviously a neat housewife.

The door was ajar and as Sheila rang the bell a voice from inside called out, 'Just dump it in the garden, I'll be out in a minute.' She heard footsteps and a child's voice chattering, 'Mummy, can I help, you promised,' followed by the abstracted reply of a busy mother, 'Yes, you can help, if you don't get in the way.'

'I didn't expect you so soon . . .' The woman's voice

trailed away as she flung open the door. 'Oh, I thought you were the man who was bringing the mushroom compost.' She was dressed in blue jeans and a T-shirt which outlined a lithe, trim figure. A mane of auburn hair had been drawn to the side of her neck and trapped in a rubber band, framing a face that, for all its harassed lines, was undeniably beautiful and bereft of make-up. A little girl clutched her trousered leg and looked up shyly at Sheila.

The woman's eyes narrowed. 'You're not from the social services?'

'No. Mrs Bailey?' said Sheila, feeling unaccountably embarrassed. She got the impression that to Esther Bailey unexpected visitors were hardly ever good news.

The woman nodded. 'Who . . . ?'

'My name's Sheila Tracy. I used to work with Harry Riley on the *Telegraph*. We were friends and he spoke of you —often,' she said quickly. Harry would surely have forgiven her that fib.

The lie did the trick. The tension drained out of Esther Bailey. She accepted Sheila's proffered hand with something approaching warmth, but surprisingly with no expression of grief or even concern.

'Uncle Harry. Uncle Harry,' burbled the little girl, chuckling delightedly to herself.

'Shush, Debbie! How is Harry? Did he ask you to call? I haven't heard from him for days. He usually gets in touch when he can. I suppose he's busy, with the job, I mean. Debbie misses him. She doesn't have many friends—round here.' Esther Bailey tossed her head dismissively in the direction of the mean little street.

For a moment Sheila was at a loss. She'd expected to be welcomed when she declared herself a friend of Harry's, but she hadn't expected that Esther wouldn't have known of his death.

The children she'd passed further up Hadley Avenue, obviously bored with playing football, had scented a more intriguing diversion and were clustering around the pavement a few feet from Esther's front door.

'I think, Mrs Bailey, it might be better if we could go inside.'

The woman looked at the children, saw her point and stepped aside for her to enter. 'It's a bit of a mess, I'm afraid. I only get the weekends for housework and the garden. I work at the check-out in Tesco's, you see. Debbie goes to play school and then my mother picks her up on weekdays.' The capsule account of her and her daughter's life came out in a rush, as if she'd learned it by rote for constant repetition to nosey neighbours and prying officials. She led Sheila into a poorly furnished but immaculately tidy front room alway from the debris of unfinished housework.

'I'll make some tea.'

'No, really, that's not necessary.'

Esther Bailey registered the note of urgency in Sheila's voice. She caught her breath. 'It's not about Martin . . . ?'

Before Sheila could reassure her, the little girl tugged fractiously at her mother's loose T-shirt, demanding attention. 'Mummy!'

'Mummy's busy, Debbie. Run along and play with Tansy. Be a good girl.'

The child demurred, then looked from her to Sheila, decided she'd be better off at her own pursuits and toddled off.

They heard her high-pitched voice from the kitchen confidentially addressing some invisible playmate. 'Now, Tansy, Mummy's busy. You must be a good girl.

Esther Bailey's anxious expression softened. 'Tansy's her doll, her pretend friend,' she explained.

'She's a lovely little girl. She's a credit to you.' Sheila felt a growing sympathy for Esther Bailey, wishing she didn't have to be the bearer of bad tidings. Good God, someone

should have told her. But then Harry had kept his past so
secret perhaps even the police didn't know of his relationship
with the Baileys.

'Miss . . . ?'

'Sheila Tracy. Sheila, please.'

The woman ignored the pleasantry. 'What is it? What
have you come to tell me.'

There was nothing for it but to be direct and honest,
however brutal it might seem.

'I hadn't realized when I came that you didn't know.
Harry's dead. He was killed when he fell from the cliff at
Seahaven. The police seem to think it was an accident. It's
happened before there.' Now was not the moment to add
her suspicion that he might have been murdered. She didn't
want to compound the distress she was already inflicting.

The woman grasped the back of a chair as if to steady
herself. She was breathing heavily, her eyes staring blankly
at the wall behind Sheila. 'I don't believe it,' she gasped,
groping for some remote possibility that the truth might
turn out to be untrue.

'Can I get you something?'

She shook her head listlessly, not yet quite comprehending
the news of Harry's death. Then she seemed to pull herself
together. She sat herself stiffly on the upright chair, her
hands primly clasped in her lap.

'When did it happen?'

'Two nights ago. Wednesday. I can't tell you how sorry
I am that you didn't know. I assumed you'd read about it
in the papers at least or heard about it on the radio.'

'I don't take the local papers or listen much to the radio.
The awful thing is I'm not really surprised. An accident,
you say?'

'Well, that's how it appears. There'll be an inquest, of
course.'

Esther Bailey managed a wry half-smile. 'Yes, I suppose
they would make it look like an accident. They're good at

that.' Suddenly, she let out a dry, rasping sob. 'It's not fair. It's never fair for people like us.'

Sheila put her arm tentatively round the woman's thin, tensed shoulders. When her gesture of compassion wasn't repulsed she tightened her grip. She felt an overwhelming sense of helplessness, but the sympathetic embrace seemed to comfort Esther Bailey. She held the keening woman in her arm for as long as it took for her to regain her composure.

'I'm all right now,' she said finally, drawing herself up with a taut dignity. 'I can't cry. I shed all the tears I have to shed when they took Martin away. You know about my husband?'

Sheila nodded. 'I know Harry thought he was innocent too.'

'He was the only one who did. Except me. Harry's belief kept me going. I didn't really think he could do anything about it or prove anything. But it was a comfort, knowing you weren't alone. Now there's no one. Just me—and Debbie. And Martin in that prison for God knows how long.'

All Stephen's warnings that she should play it cool and noncommittal fled from Sheila's mind. In the face of Esther Bailey's controlled grief she knew only that she wanted to declare herself an ally.

'Mrs Bailey. Esther. You're *not* alone. I don't know all the facts of the case against your husband. But I knew Harry and since his death I'm beginning to understand a lot of things that—well, frankly, I never even thought about before. I realize it's hard for you now, but if you could talk to me I want to help.'

Esther Bailey looked up at her strangely. 'Why? You're not Harry's kind. You're from their side.'

'That's what I used to think. But not any more. I've learned a good deal about myself in the last couple of days. All I know is that Harry died for a reason. I don't think it was an accident either. And I want to find out what that reason was and if in the process it proves your husband's innocence that's a bonus.' The conviction with which she spoke didn't fool her. It was partly bravado, partly the need to gain Esther Bailey's confidence, and somewhere too a belief that justice should be done, although she'd have felt embarrassed putting that pious sentiment into words.

'I can see why Harry would have rated you,' Esther said with wary admiration. 'You've got spunk. You don't look it, but you have. But how do I know I can trust you? You work for a paper. How do I know you don't just want another story? Come to think of it, I didn't know Harry let on to anyone in Seahaven that he was related to Martin.'

Having been caught out in the lie with which she'd introduced herself, Sheila blushed. To be less than straightforward now would be an insult to Esther Bailey. 'You're right. I didn't know Harry was Martin Bailey's cousin until I got hold of his diary after his death and talked to a man named Joe Slack in Brighton who'd been doing some investigating, so he said, for Harry. And you're right again, you don't know if you can trust me. You'll just have to take my word for it.'

The woman regarded Sheila for a long moment, weighing up her words. 'What can I lose!' she said at last. 'What is it you want to know? It's all on the record. The trial was reported in the papers along with all those snide articles afterwards about how Martin had served time. He was eighteen. A couple of so-called mates had talked him into being lookout when they nicked a load of cigarettes from a lorry. When he was caught they left him holding the bag. He served six months, but when he came out he swore he'd stay clean. That's when he met me and we got married. After that, he was straight as a die. Hard working, a good provider and the best of husbands. But they didn't bother to report that. Once a crook, always a crook. If he was capable of making one stupid mistake when he was eighteen he was capable of murder and arson,' she said bitterly.

'I'm not interested in what's on the record, Esther. I want to know what didn't go on the record. First, tell me about Harry and your husband. Cousins aren't usually so close.'

Esther closed her eyes, remembering, perhaps trying to exorcize, this new grief. 'Martin practically brought Harry up. He was twelve years older. Harry's parents had died in a car crash when he was a kid. They were going to send him to a children's home, but Martin took him in. We'd just got married. Even then the authorities weren't happy, what with Martin's being a convicted felon. But they came round in the end and Harry moved in with us.'

'Harry idolized Martin,' she went on. 'And for a while it seemed I couldn't have a child, so I was glad to have him too. He was a good kid, fast learner, clever. He could be a bit wild, but Martin always knew how to handle him. He did well at school and when he left he got himself a job as a sort of messenger on the *Brighton Argus*. He always had a flair for writing and he was determined not to stay an office boy for long. Martin was really proud of him.'

'What did your husband do? I mean, what job?'

'Would you believe it, he was a gardener. Maintenance gardening. That didn't come out in the papers either. They said he was an odd job man. He'd always had a yen for working in the outdoors and one of the prison visitors urged him to take up gardening—as a profession—when he came out. He recommended him to a local nurseryman who gave him a chance. Martin made good, then set up on his own in a small way. He built up a nice little business. Slowly but surely. He was reliable and good. There's not much call for gardeners around here. But he used to advertise in the personal columns and got quite a few jobs. In Hove, Brighton, even up your way in Seahaven. He had a van, you see, and could travel.'

'You wouldn't happen to know where he worked in Seahaven or for whom?'

Esther shook her head. 'I've no idea. It was just a job— a big job. Paving, landscaping. He was on it a couple of weeks. But, so far as I was concerned, they were just clients. If he mentioned names, I didn't register them.'

'And, of course, all this was before the fire at the ware-house?'

'Naturally. It was a couple of days after the fire that they took Martin in for questioning and then they charged him.'

'On what evidence?'

Esther plucked at a loose thread in her jeans nervously. 'Do you really want me to go over all that again?'

'Please.'

'Martin knew the boys in the fire. He knew they were pushers. Drugs. A pal of his had been an addict and died of it. He'd caught them trying to nobble kids outside the local school and had a flaming row with them. Threatened to turn them in.'

'Why didn't he?'

'Miss Tracy, I can see you've never been on the wrong side of the law. If you had, you wouldn't ask. You keep your distance from the police. If Martin had shopped them, they'd either have sworn he was involved or the bogies would have drawn that conclusion themselves.'

'That's plain stupid.'

It came out more righteously than Sheila had intended but surprisingly Esther didn't take exception. 'I know—now. Maybe it would have made all the difference if he had gone to the police. But at the time I could understand how he felt and he seemed to have scared the kids rotten. He had a temper and he was—is—a big chap. Probably he felt they were too young to go through what he'd gone through with the law. But it's easy to be wise after the event. How could he know a few weeks later they'd be burnt to death in a fire.'

'How public was the row he had with the boys?'

'Just about as public as you could get, short of broadcast-ing it on television. There were plenty of witnesses ready to testify about it. And then it all seemed to pile up. Martin had bought petrol on the night of the fire from a nearby garage. It was for his lawn-mower, but he couldn't prove that. And a nice neighbour—' the tone of her voice indicated that the neighbour was anything but 'nice'—'saw Martin passing the warehouse ten minutes or so before it started to blaze. They found a rake of his ditched by the warehouse door after the fire. He'd mislaid it days before or maybe someone had nicked it. Anyway, it wasn't important and he forgot about it. But when the police faced him with it he got scared and denied it was his. That made him look bad—like everything else.'

'But no real, hard proof.'

'I don't know about that. The prosecution made it all sound pretty convincing in court. Even the solicitor I saw when he was first charged thought so. He said he'd see Martin and the police and look into it. But then the next day he'd got some trumped-up reason why he wouldn't touch the case or suggest a lawyer we could afford. We didn't have much money, so the court appointed a legal aid man for Martin. Neither of us had much faith in him and I suppose he didn't have much faith in Martin.'

'Who was the solicitor you went to first?'

'Just a chap who'd drawn up a contract for a job of maintenance work between Martin and one of his clients. He was the only solicitor I knew of. He had a practice in Brighton at the time but not any more. Someone called Blythe.'

'Edgar?'

'Could be. Are you all right?'

Sheila took a deep breath. 'I'm all right.' She hadn't been aware that she'd reacted so strongly. Edgar Blythe! It all came back to Seahaven.

CHAPTER 12

'Mummy, Tansy's naughty. I smacked her.'

The plaintive voice jerked both women back into the present from the painfully remembered past.

A tear trickled down the woebegone little face in the doorway. 'I'm hungry!' A small foot stamped on the floor.

Esther Bailey cast a guilty, don't-say-anything look at Sheila, who nodded reassuringly.

'I'll just settle her,' she said. 'You forget . . . little pigs! Come on, Debbie. What's a big girl like you doing, crying? I'll give Tansy a good talking to. Then you can have a big bowl of wheaties. You like wheaties.'

'And an apple!'

'And an apple.'

'And an ice lolly,' Debbie burbled on, pushing her luck.

'Maybe this afternoon. When we go shopping. I won't be a minute,' Esther called over her shoulder as she shooed her daughter back into the kitchen.

With half an ear Sheila listened to Debbie's seemingly endless catalogue of Tansy's misdemeanours punctuated by her mother's soothing responses, but her mind was elsewhere. If she'd had any doubts before, Esther's story had dispelled them. Whatever the results of the inquest, she was convinced now that Harry's death was no accident. But proving it was something else. Even the fact that Esther had approached Edgar Blythe and he'd turned her down when he'd been in practice in Brighton was evidence of nothing but Blythe's bigoted refusal to soil his hands or his reputation with such a case, especially as there would be no fat fee in prospect. And that wasn't news. It was well known that the poor got short shrift from Edgar Blythe. It was almost a joke, except it didn't seem so funny now.

No wonder Harry had taken such a delight in exposing the shortcomings of Edgar and his equally reactionary wife Marion.

'That'll keep her quiet for a while,' said Esther when she returned. 'I don't know how I'll tell her. She adored Harry so.'

As she lit up a cigarette her hands were shaking. 'I'm not

enjoying this. I've tried to put it behind me. What's the use? It won't bring Martin back, will it? Honestly?'

'Honestly, I don't know. But if we could just find something to justify reopening the case.' Somehow Sheila had to make this defeated woman feel there was still some hope.

'There was an appeal, but they just went over the same thing again and came to the same conclusion. And Martin's still there, wasting his life away.'

'Did your husband keep books, accounts?' It was a dubious point. Sheila suspected that at least some of his transactions would have been cash on the nail which wouldn't have shown up in his tax returns. All the same, you couldn't run a business, however small, without accounts.

Esther flushed. 'He wasn't very good at the paper work. But he had to keep some records for VAT and so on.'

'What happened to them?'

'Debbie and I stayed with my mother during the trial and quite a while afterwards. When we came back here someone had broken in and gone through the place. They took a few little bits, nothing of value—we didn't have anything like that. All the drawers were turned out. I told the police, but what could they do? They said it had probably been a sneak thief, kids maybe, seeing as how the house had been unoccupied for so long. It wasn't until much later that I realized Martin's account books had gone too. But it didn't seem to matter much. Nothing mattered much.'

'So you didn't inform the police?'

'Miss Tracy, by that time I'd had the police up to here.' She sliced her hand in a cutting gesture across her throat.

Sheila sighed. Every lead seemed to run into a cul-de-sac.

'What did your husband remember about the night of the fire?'

'Just what came out in the trial. That's the swine of it. It was all true. He *did* have a rumpus with those kids. He *did* buy petrol. He *was* walking past the warehouse a few minutes before.'

'And he didn't see anything unusual or suspicious then?'

'You don't go around looking for anything unusual or suspicious, as you put it, when you're walking quite innocently home at night. There were some cars parked near. But there are always cars parked everywhere. And he thought he saw a couple of people in one.'

'Well, surely, if the police asked for witnesses they came forward.'

Esther shook her head. 'If they had, maybe Martin wouldn't be in gaol now. And he couldn't identify the car or the make, so naturally they didn't believe him.' She was talking rapidly, barely concealing her irritation. She supposed, thought Sheila, her questions were like salt rubbed into a still open wound.

'Please bear with me. I know it's painful.'

'How can you know? You've never been through it,' the woman said bitterly.

Sheila swallowed the rebuke. 'How far from here is the warehouse? Was it a regular walk for him?'

'Maybe once, twice a week on the way back from the pub where he played darts. It's just a bit along the coast. Where that new leisure complex is. Bar, disco. The company that owned the land sold it up cheap after the fire to some property speculator. I try not to pass it now, but when I do it gives me the creeps.' She shivered.

'And all the time since the trial Harry had been trying to get evidence to prove your husband innocent?'

'Harry never gave up. I tried to believe in what he was doing, but after a while I couldn't. It all seemed so useless.'

'You knew about this man Slack who was supposed to be helping him?'

'I knew and I didn't like it. I told Harry he was just a con man. But Harry thought he might find out something the police couldn't.'

'But how did he get the money to pay Slack?'

'Oh, don't worry, he didn't hold up a bank. He worked. After his job at the *Argus*, he did anything that would bring in a few quid. Bartender, waiter, bouncer. He hardly spent a penny on himself. When he went to Seahaven I hoped that was the end of it. I was glad for him. It was such a good opening. He deserved something better than spending his life worrying about Martin and Debbie and me.'

'I don't suppose he'd have thought that, Esther. From what you've told me he owed Martin a lot.'

'And he paid his dues, didn't he? In the worst way.'

Sheila nodded. A different Harry was emerging from her talk with Esther Bailey. She couldn't believe that the image of brash, artful muck-raker was a front. That was Harry. It was part of his nature. He couldn't be otherwise. But there was another side to him, loyal, caring, that no one on the *Telegraph*, not even she, had suspected. She remembered Alec's joking remarks about his padded expenses and they'd all thought that was just typical of him, making a bit extra on the side. Most journalists were adept at producing creative expenses. None of them knew or would probably have believed that every spare pound went into the pocket of Joe Slack.

The next time Debbie put in an appearance munching her apple, Sheila realized she couldn't decently impose on Esther Bailey any longer.

The woman saw her to the door. The children were still idly kicking their football up the street. 'I suppose I should thank you—for bothering,' she said. 'But somehow I can't. You'll let me know about Harry. The funeral. I should . . .'

'Don't worry. The paper will pay the expenses.' And if they don't, I will, thought Sheila, as the front door was shut firmly behind her, leaving Esther Bailey to get on with her lonely, left-over life.

She walked briskly down Hadley Avenue, dodging a well-aimed football and avoiding the curious eyes of the children. As she turned on to the coast road she had the prickling sensation that she was being followed. It was lunch-time and relatively quiet. At first she tried to shrug it off. Over-reacting again. But the feeling persisted. It wasn't a pedestrian. The only footsteps she could hear were her own. But then her ears became attuned to the low purr of a car, crawling along the kerbside, keeping pace behind her. She forced herself not to run, not to look back, but as she quickened her pace, so too did the car. She didn't notice a rut in the pavement and, before she could save herself, she stumbled and fell awkwardly. She heard a car door open and slam and felt two powerful arms cupping themselves round her waist and pulling her to her feet. She struggled against them but the arms were too strong for her.

As she lashed behind her with her shoulder-bag a restraining hand tugged it away from her. Good God, I'm being mugged! The moment the thought flashed through her mind, a familiar voice brought her to her senses. 'Hold on. It's only me.'

She shrugged herself free of the vice-like grip, grabbed back her bag and looked round into the amused, leering eyes of Jack Murray. 'Just helping a lady in distress.' He held up his arms in a mocking gesture of surrender. 'I'd always fancied a wrestling match with you, but in rather cosier circumstances.' He stood there laughing. The engine of his sleek, grey metallic Mercedes was still dutifully purring away a few feet away.

Feeling silly, she made a futile effort to brush the dust and dirt of the pavement from her skirt, surveying the hole in her tights through which an ugly graze was seeping blood.

'Here.' He produced a clean handkerchief which she snatched angrily and applied to the graze.

'You scared the life out of me. I thought you were a mugger.'

'I've been called a lot of things in my time, but I haven't yet stooped to mugging.'

'Then why were you following me?'

'Curious. What's a nice girl like you doing in this neck of the woods?'

He'd been drinking, not a lot, but just enough to explain his air of bravado. Not that Jack Murray was exactly the diffident type. But, apart from his outburst at the meeting the previous evening, he usually managed to control himself in Seahaven, shrewdly tailoring his personality to the company he kept—or, at least, the company he wished to impress.

She ignored his implication that there was anything strange about her being seen in the neighbourhood of Shoreham harbour.

'I could ask you the same thing.'

'Business.' She knew that Jack Murray's interests ranged far along the Sussex coast. She wished she had as plausible an explanation. She certainly didn't intend to tell Jack Murray the purpose of her visit.

'Just—on a job,' she volunteered lamely.

'Pretty far from home.'

'News doesn't begin and end in Seahaven, you know. Even for the *Telegraph*.'

He looked at her speculatively as if weighing up what she'd said and, more probably, what she hadn't said. He started to speak, then stopped abruptly. 'At least let me drive you wherever you want to go. That knee doesn't look too healthy to me.'

She wavered for a moment and he laughed again. 'I promise, both hands on the wheel.'

The knee was beginning to throb and she didn't fancy the walk back to her car. 'Thanks,' she conceded grudgingly. 'If you could just drop me in Hove.'

'No sooner said.' He opened the door of the passenger seat and waved her in with an exaggerated show of courtesy.

Only as they were driving the short distance to Hove did she wonder to herself about the precise nature of Jack Murray's business in Shoreham.

*

The first performance of *Punk Lust* was due to start in half an hour at the Palace when Stephen Gough arrived.

Already a few customers were lurking around the foyer of the cinema. The film had been roundly condemned by most of the critics when it was first shown in London as an outrageous affront to public decency. A verdict that instantly insured it box office success wherever it was screened in the country.

The usherette hadn't yet come on duty, but the cashier was checking the confectionery, soft drinks and popcorn stall in the foyer. She was a round, middle-aged woman whose sharp tongue belied her docile appearance. Observing Stephen out of the corner of her eye, she snapped 'Not open yet' at him without bothering to turn round.

'I don't want to see the film,' he said quickly.

'Don't blame you. Load of rubbish if you ask me. I've seen worse on the beach on a hot Saturday night.'

'I just wanted to ask you a couple of questions.'

This time she did turn round. 'I'm not taking part in any survey. What they show here is up to the manager. I just work here.'

'And very efficiently, I'm sure.' He smiled charmingly at the dumpy woman with the calculated guile he'd learned from past years of coaxing information out of unwilling interviewees.

Faced with such an ingratiating customer, she preened herself a little, enjoying an attention she didn't often receive.

'I do my best,' she sniffed, but less tartly than before.

'I'm not interested in a survey. I'm a reporter on the case of that young man who died at Seahaven a couple of nights ago.' It was, after all, only half a lie. 'We want to follow up the events that happened before he had the accident. Just background stuff, you understand. You do recall it?'

'The police were here, weren't they? How couldn't I recall it?'

'The usherette identified him. Harry Riley.'

'Only because there'd been a bit of a barney here weeks ago between him and some other lads in the foyer. Nasty little bleeders! Mavis remembered she'd heard his name then and she'd shown him to a seat in the back row the other night and when she learned about his death from the local radio she told the police. Keeps up with what's going on, does Mavis.'

'Did you remember seeing him?'

'Only from his picture in the paper. Then I remembered.'

'Did he come in with anyone?'

'I wouldn't know about that. We were so busy, you see. Queues at night.'

'Were there any unusual patrons that night?'

'What do you mean—unusual?'

'Not the kind of people you get for a film like *Punk Lust*.'

'Oh, we get all kinds. Women too. You'd be surprised.'

Stephen sighed. He had just arrived at the conclusion that he'd better hang around for Mavis-who-kept-up-with-what's-going-on when the cashier interrupted, 'Hang about. There was one chap. It was his shoes. I'm very fussy about shoes. Can always tell a really good pair of shoes. And his hands, very well groomed. I'm fussy about hands, too.'

'What was so peculiar about that?'

'The rest of him. His clothes. Seedy. Muffler. Dirty old mac. We get a lot of dirty macs. I wouldn't have paid any mind, until I spotted the shoes and the hands when he paid his money.'

'Almost as if the mac and muffler were a camouflage.' He was putting words into her mouth. She thought for a moment and then adopted them as her own.

'That's right. Sort of camouflage. It hadn't struck me before.'

'You didn't see him leave? Or Harry Riley?'

She shook her head regretfully. She'd like to have accommodated this attractive man but, in her own way, she was a truthful woman. 'I just didn't think about him—until now.'

'You've been very helpful, Mrs . . . ?'

'Bright. Bright by name and bright by nature. Divorced. Well—separated. He scarpered years ago.' She touched her dyed blonde hair and sucked in her plump cheeks, wanting to look more tempting than she knew she was.

'He must have been mad,' Stephen assured her. 'I'm very grateful.'

As he turned to go she called after him. 'I could sneak you in. You wouldn't have to pay.'

He smiled back at her. 'Another time, perhaps.'

She watched him leave, past the stragglers who were waiting for the cinema to open. 'It always is another time,' she murmured to herself, then shrugged and busied herself with the display of Mars bars and Bounties.

CHAPTER 13

'Here, try this,' Andrew Tracy greeted Sheila. The amber liquid looked enticing enough in one of the Waterford crystal goblets the staff had given him when he retired from the bank. But, from experience, she eyed it dubiously.

'What is it? Gooseberry, melon and ginger or potato peelings?' Andrew's attempts at wine-making had grown increasingly more inventive as the hobby had become an obsession, with occasionally explosive results when bottles had blown their tops. The kitchen had smelt like a brewery for days afterwards.

'Just taste it.'

She took a sip. 'Not bad.'

'Not bad! A triumph. What happened to you?'

She'd almost forgotten her grazed knee as she'd mulled over her conversation with Esther Bailey on the drive home from Shoreham. She hesitated before answering. 'I tripped.'

'Oh yes. You've been doing a lot of that lately, haven't you?' he replied, meaning more than he said, but not wanting to push her for a fuller explanation. In her good time, she'd confide in him. 'I should put some salve on it.'

'Thanks for the sympathy. You don't suppose I could have a decent glass of sherry?'

He sighed. 'You just don't appreciate the wine-makers' art.' But he poured her a glass of the decent sherry and watched, concerned, as she drank half of it gratefully. 'Bad day?'

'Sort of. I asked Steve to look in. Can we rustle up an extra lamb chop?'

'I already have. Steve phoned me just before you got back.'

She shook her head at him over the rim of her glass, pique and pleasure equally matched. 'You two!'

'John Agnew phoned too.'

'What did he want?'

'You don't have to sound so suspicious. He's still fond of you.'

There'd been a time when Sheila and John Agnew had been sufficiently involved for Seahaven to anticipate a wedding. He'd seemed so eminently suitable: a youngish widower with two small, amenable children. He was well-heeled, successful, pleasant and, above all, nice. A perfect match for pleasant, nice Sheila. It would have been a safe, sensible, secure marriage. When, after the occasional dinner dance, they'd quite naturally gone to bed together, they'd even enjoyed an agreeable sexual relationship.

She couldn't explain why she withdrew from committing herself to John Agnew and Andrew hadn't asked, although he regretted it for her sake. Maybe a small part of her, deep down and not fully understood even by herself, rebelled against becoming a comfortable cog in the Seahaven social scene for the rest of her life. Love didn't really enter into it. Love, she'd decided, was a fantasy that had long since passed her by. Only now did she realize that love was the turmoil of emotion, the feeling of suspense, she felt in the company of Stephen Gough.

'Do I sound suspicious?' She supposed she did. John Agnew was, after all, a member of the Seahaven establishment she'd come to distrust.

'He just wanted to know if you'd care to join him at the next Rotary ladies' night.'

'I wonder why. He hasn't asked me out for ages.'

'The trouble with you, my girl, is that you're developing distinct signs of paranoia.'

'With good cause, wouldn't you think? After that warning last night. Dad, Steve and I, want to pump you. You won't go all bank manager, confidence of clients, on us, will you?'

'Pump me? You sound as if you've been reading too many Raymond Chandler thrillers.'

She held out her glass for another sherry. 'Right now I feel as if I'm living in a Raymond Chandler thriller and I don't like it.'

He plumped his bulky body, incongruously encased in a plastic kitchen apron with the words 'Local Hero' stamped on the surface, beside her on the settee. With that surprising gentleness of very big men, he placed a hand on her grazed knee. 'I know what you've been going through, Sheila, believe me.'

She stared seriously at the huge hand with its delicate touch. 'Steve says I'm over-reacting. I keep repeating that bloody word. Am I?'

'Probably a bit. Give it up, Sheila,' he said earnestly.

She frowned, puzzled. 'But it was you . . .'

'I know. I didn't realize how deeply you'd get involved.'

'I can't now.'

He searched her face anxiously. 'No, I suppose you can't. But no good will come of it.' He was silent for a moment and she had the impression he was wrestling with some inner conflict. Then he recovered the genial urbanity which, for the first time in her life, seemed to her forced and somehow out of true. 'Enough said. Wash up. And I promise I won't burden you with my superb elderberry wine at dinner. You can have a rotten old vintage burgundy from the off licence.'

She laughed. He could always turn a drama into a farce.

'What a good little provider you are. Mother would have been proud.'

'She is. Don't think just because you can't see them any more they're not keeping tabs on us all down here.'

By the time Stephen arrived after a confidential chat with Inspector Jimmy Grant her good humour was restored. As she busied herself in the kitchen she heard him making polite noises about the new wine her father had insisted that Stephen sample. She enjoyed listening to the low murmur of easy conversation between the two men. She wished that things could remain just as they were at that moment, an isolated pocket of time that would last forever. 'But wishing won't make it so,' she muttered.

'Are you hungry?' She poked her head through the hatch from the kitchen, her face flushed from the heat of the cooker. 'What's wrong?' Steve was studying her intently.

'I was just thinking how nice you look.'

She grinned. 'Nice! Ugh! I've a good mind to clout you with a lamb chop.'

It wasn't until after they'd eaten, finished the bottle of good burgundy and were drinking the perked coffee that Andrew brought up the subject Sheila had been delaying. By an unspoken agreement both she and Stephen knew he'd get around to it after the pleasantries. But he couldn't be pushed. There was a time for everything.

'Sheila tells me you want to pump me.' He accented the word 'pump' elaborately. She'd already told him about her encounter with Esther Bailey and Jack Murray, her appointment with Joe Slack, while Stephen had given them a light-hearted account of his visit to the Palace. Although he'd kept to himself what had passed between him and Jimmy Grant.

'What do you know about Eleanor Rushton? You go back a long way. I know she was one of the bank's customers.' From experience she knew it was better to plunge straight into the deep end with her father.

He chewed over her question for a moment. 'I see what you mean about the confidence of clients.'

'Dad, I'm not asking for a bank loan or information for the Inland Revenue.'

He nodded. 'Ask away. If it's fair, I'll answer.'

'Her daughter?'

Andrew hesitated, then seemed to arrive at a decision. 'It's really no particular secret, I suppose. It's just a long time ago. I doubt whether many people remember. Sarah, the daughter, was born two years after her husband died.'

'Illegitimate?'

'I think you can safely say that.' Andrew smiled. There was an old-fashioned streak in his daughter that always amused him. 'I thought these days they called them one parent families.'

'So Sarah and Nicholas are half-brother and sister. It must have caused a mild scandal in Seahaven.'

'Hardly. A few raised eyebrows. Eleanor Rushton, even when she was much younger, was a strong, independent-minded woman. She didn't allow it to be a scandal. She conducted herself impeccably. The child was born. And, like the Duchess of Windsor, she never explained and never complained. She didn't need to. It was assumed that the father was a local man or he might have been one of her husband's friends. But her position in Seahaven society was established enough for her to ride any rumours and certainly her generosity to local causes was an asset the community wouldn't lightly wish to jeopardize. After a while people forgot about the girl's parentage. They do, you know. She was just part of the family. I doubt whether Eleanor Rushton has given the subject any thought from the time the baby was christened. Brandy, Steve?'

Stephen shook his head. 'I wonder why she didn't marry the man. Or any man, come to that. She's a very handsome woman. A young, rich widow. There must have been plenty of likely contenders.'

'Your guess is as good as mine.'

'I don't think so. Your guess would be better. On second thoughts, yes please to brandy. It's not your own creation, is it?' he added nervously.

'That,' said Andrew as he produced three brandy globes and poured ample measures into them from the decanter, 'is in the experimental stage.' The exercise gave him time to weigh his words which was precisely what Stephen had intended.

'Under the terms of her husband's will she inherited everything. The house, the money, the farm. He was a lot older than her. He'd made his money in the City, lucrative takeover deals and so on. Then he'd taken early retirement and become a gentleman farmer—that is, he owned the farm and employed a capable staff to run it. For the rest of his life he devoted himself to local charities. A tradition, may I remind you again, that his widow has kept up.'

'Amazing how philanthropic financiers become after they've made their pile!'

Andrew ignored Sheila's acid remark. Her views on the ethics of big business were well known and hotly argued. It was one of the few issues about which, in the past, she'd been prepared to stand up and be counted, her habitual fear of giving offence deserting her.

'Had she remarried she'd have retained title to the house and received a decent but not extravagant allowance,' Andrew continued. 'But the bulk of the estate would have been held in trust for her son Nicholas until he reached the age of twenty-one.'

'So, if the man were penniless she'd have lost out by marrying him.'

'Crudely put, my dear. But roughly right. Mind you, I'm merely supposing that was a reason for her not remarrying. Perhaps she just prefers to remain her own mistress.'

'And perhaps someone else's—on the quiet?'

'What a devious mind you're developing.'

'Don't put on that holier-than-thou attitude, Dad. It must have crossed your mind.'

'Why should it? From everything I've seen and heard, Eleanor Rushton's life has been as open and respectable as the Queen Mother's.'

'All the same, she was capable of one little peccadillo.'

'Nearly twenty years ago when she was recently widowed! I can't believe you're that bigoted, Sheila.'

Sheila felt herself getting increasingly angry with her father. 'You're deliberately misunderstanding me. I don't care if she's had affairs from here to—to Timbuctoo. That's her business. *My* business is trying to find out why Harry Riley was killed. No, don't let's be prissy about it. Murdered!'

'Calm down, Sheila.' Stephen put his hand on hers. 'Your father's only trying to put things in perspective.'

'Why are you both so damned reasonable all of a sudden?' she flared.

The two men exchanged pained glances but remained silent. They didn't have to speak. She thought she knew why they were behaving so rationally. Although she wasn't yet ready to admit it. They were concerned for her. Harry's death had become a personal crusade and the intensity of her feelings about it was alarming them. It alarmed her, too, but for a different reason.

'Look, promise, calm,' she said finally. 'It's not just Harry. A man is languishing in Parkhurst . . .'

'For a crime he's been convicted for committing,' Stephen reminded her.

'If you'd heard Esther Bailey you'd have doubts too. Innocent men do get sent mistakenly to prison.'

'Granted. But you're not going to help him or Esther

Bailey or anyone else by flying off the handle and accusing everyone right, left and centre of being implicated. If you go around waving a flag you're not going to find out anything. Anyway, there's one other thing I'd like to know, Andrew. What happened to the daughter after she was raped?'

'Officially, Eleanor sent her abroad to stay with relatives in Switzerland. I believe she's still at school or college over there. She'd be about eighteen now.'

'And unofficially?'

'I've no reason to doubt that isn't the truth.'

Sheila had the feeling that he knew more than he was telling. But she knew if he didn't wish to be drawn proverbial wild horses wouldn't drag it out of him. Like everyone else, he had his secret places which were inviolate.

'It must have been a horrible experience for a girl like her,' she said quietly. 'Enough to make her mother hate her son for not taking proper care of Sarah that night, wouldn't you say?'

The shrill ring of the telephone made her jump. 'Blast! It's probably John. I'll get it.'

When she returned from the hall after taking the call she stood in the doorway, a look of amazement on her face.

'She must be telepathic.'

'Who?'

'Eleanor Rushton. It was her on the phone. She's asked me if I could spare the time to call at her house tomorrow morning.'

CHAPTER 14

'How very good of you to call, my dear.' Eleanor Rushton managed to make it sound as if the visit was not of her instigation but an unexpected pleasure.

She knows how to catch you left-footed, thought Sheila, as the demure parlourmaid ushered her into the spacious conservatory overlooking the neatly manicured lawns of Oakley Hall and the wide, loping sweep of the South Downs in the distance.

'If it's too hot for you here . . .'

Sheila shook her head.

'I'm a chilly mortal myself and I love the view.' Eleanor Rushton waved her to a cane chair. 'Coffee or perhaps a drink?'

'No, I'm fine. You wanted to see me.' While admiring the ease with which Mrs Rushton took command of the game she was playing, whatever that game might be, Sheila was determined to lob the ball back into her corner of the court. She'd been well primed by her father and Stephen to keep a cool head, but that didn't mean she had to defer to all Eleanor Rushton's little niceties for the sake of good manners.

'Yes, I did, didn't I?' said Mrs Rushton, as if reminding herself of a surprising aberration. She arranged herself gracefully on the low lounger chair opposite Sheila. 'I felt there was a certain amount of—how shall I put it?—acrimony at the meeting the other evening.'

'You mean some of us lost our temper.'

An attractive gurgle, too contained to be a chuckle, greeted Sheila's down-to-earth assessment of the fraught Festival meeting.

'I think we were all a little overwrought. It was very upsetting hearing about that poor boy's death and maybe some people felt just a wee bit guilty about . . .'

' . . . about slagging him off in the past.' It was an ugly expression, deliberately chosen by Sheila in an effort to dent the woman's composure. She failed.

'I wouldn't put it that roughly,' said Eleanor Rushton as if ticking off a cheeky schoolgirl. 'I just felt I didn't want you to get the wrong idea.'

'Oh, I don't think I got the wrong idea, Mrs Rushton.'

She's testing me, trying to find out how much I know about Harry. Sheila waited patiently for the mistress of Oakley Hall to continue, but when she did she found herself caught off-guard again.

'Incidentally, Miss Tracy, I haven't yet thanked you for sparing your Sunday morning like this. I know how precious weekends are when you're a working girl.' Sheila smiled. It was an awfully good act. She doubted whether Mrs Rushton even remembered what it was like to be a working girl, if she ever had been.

'So, I won't waste your time. I really wanted to talk about the Festival this year. I was wondering whether you'd take a more active part in the arrangements. I was discussing you with Ida Glaxton and the others.' I just bet you were, thought Sheila. 'And we thought if you'd agree to coordinate the parade through the town of the local youth organizations it would be a great help.'

She leaned marginally forward, confidentially, gesticulating with a surprisingly workmanlike hand. 'Strictly between you and me, Ida Glaxton is no match for the leaders of the various groups who all have their own ideas. I think you'd be much more likely to get them to agree to a common theme. They would respond to someone younger and more vital.'

'I don't imagine Mrs Glaxton would take too kindly to my interference.' The invitation had taken the wind out of Sheila's sails. It was the last thing she'd expected from her meeting with Eleanor Rushton. It occurred to her that maybe she had misjudged the woman, maybe quite genuinely all she wanted was an extra pair of hands in organizing the Festival. In which case she'd be in for a disappointment.

'Oh, Ida's very amenable. She realizes she takes on too much and then can't quite cope. But I know I can rely on your discretion not to quote me.'

Sheila gritted her teeth. The visit wasn't going at all as she'd anticipated. 'Of course you can rely on my discretion.

But I'm afraid you can't rely on my help. The paper does keep me very busy, unsocial hours and so on. As you said, working girls!' At least, she'd get that dig in.

The smile on Eleanor Rushton's face froze glassily but just for an instant. She wasn't used to being thwarted but was too well bred to show it.

'Well, of course, if that's how you feel, I understand. Far better not to take something on if you can't devote sufficient time to it. Although I must say I'm disappointed. You seem so—so *involved* in everything that happens in Seahaven.'

There was the merest suggestion of an underlying meaning in the way she stressed her remark.

'Anyway, now that I've brought you out here you must let me give you some refreshment.' Eleanor Rushton seemed to dismiss the episode from her mind and Sheila doubted whether she could be bothered now to give her the time of day, let alone refreshment.

'No, I should be going. Thank you all the same.'

Eleanor Rushton rose from her chair with a touch too much alacrity and guided Sheila from the conservatory into the adjacent morning-room, its air of formality as pronounced as the withering courtesy of its owner. Only a sunny flower arrangement on a low table flanking the photograph of a pale, mousey young girl with intense deep-set eyes, softened the impersonal decor of the room.

'I've enjoyed our little talk.' Mrs Rushton held out a limp hand. 'We must do it again sometime.' Then she paused, a slight frown creasing the shell-like, unlined forehead as if she were wrestling with a decision she wasn't sure whether she should make.

Grasping Sheila's elbow as she propelled her towards the front door, she said almost as an afterthought, 'By the way, I was interested to hear of that boy's concern about the warehouse fire in Shoreham. Frightful business. I never thought that man got a fair trial. Perhaps he didn't either. Harry Riley, I mean.'

You really are a cunning customer, Sheila mused, dropping it into the conversation just like that.

'I wouldn't have thought you'd remember very much about it, Mrs Rushton. After all, it was several years ago. A good many crimes have been committed locally since then.'

She felt the woman tighten her grip on her arm as she swung Sheila round to face her. Her clear blue eyes were staring so directly into hers that she felt compelled to look away.

'Come, Miss Tracy. I'm sure you know very well why I would follow the trial. One of the teenagers who died in the fire was the boy who raped my daughter. I should think that would be sufficient reason for my interest in it. Just because I don't talk about it doesn't mean I don't still feel strongly about the harm he did to Sarah. I suppose I even felt glad when I heard of his death. The law let him off so lightly. But then I realized that harbouring grudges is a fruitless and destructive exercise.'

There was no doubting her sincerity. The gracious lady mask had yielded to the anguished expression of a mother whose child had been cruelly abused.

The sympathy she felt for the woman's obvious distress overrode Sheila's previous supicions about Eleanor Rushton's motive in inviting her to call. She'd seen that look only the day before in the eyes of Esther Bailey as she recalled the circumstances that had led to her husband's conviction for arson and murder. And she'd reacted just as strongly then.

'I'm sorry. I know how you must feel.' She'd said that before, too, or words to that effect. And she detected the same accusing response in Eleanor Rushton as she'd received from Esther Bailey. How can you know? You haven't been through it.

'I hope . . . your daughter . . .' The unspoken question hung for a moment, limp and unfocused, between them.

Then Mrs Rushton drew herself up and rearranged her expression. The mask came down again, a kind of fortress, protecting her emotions from casual prying.

'She's very well, thank you. Fortunately the young are very resilient,' she elaborated. But her words were as meaningless as her polite pleasantries. The subject was resolutely closed. It would have taken a far more insensitive soul than Sheila to dare to re-open it.

'It's a pity you haven't time to see the garden,' said Mrs Rushton with the polite firmness which clearly wasn't about to brook any suggestion that Sheila might indeed find the time after all. 'It's always so lovely in the late spring and early summer.'

The idle remark struck a chord of memory in Sheila. 'Did Martin Bailey, the man who was convicted, ever work for you, Mrs Rushton?' She remembered Esther had mentioned he had been engaged on a big job in Seahaven. Apart from a municipal contract, Oakley Hall was the only estate around likely to need outside help. Most Seahaven residents managed their own gardens or made do with local jobbing gardeners.

Eleanor Rushton's reply was franker than she'd expected. 'As a matter of fact, he did. It was about a week's work, maybe more. There was a lot of cutting back to be done and I wanted to lay a path in the rose-garden. It was too much for Yates, my gardener. Bailey came with a good recommendation from a nurseryman we deal with. His rates were fair and he did an excellent job.'

She's telling me too much, thought Sheila. Why?

'I don't suppose you saw Martin Bailey after that?'

'Why on earth should I? Naturally I read that he'd been arrested later and it surprised me. But I had very little to do with him. I left it to Yates. He seemed a quiet, reliable man. But then you can't judge anyone on such a flimsy acquaintanceship, can you, Miss Tracy?'

Again, there was that uncomfortable note of challenge in

her voice. If she pushed too far, Sheila felt Eleanor Rushton
was quite capable of having her unceremoniously booted
out of the door.

She smiled. 'No, I suppose not.' Mrs Rushton continued
to regard her with cool hostility.

The roar of a motorbike in the drive fractured the icy
atmosphere between the two women. The change in Eleanor
Rushton was remarkable. The hostility was replaced with
anger, her natural composure visibly draining away. She
glanced nervously at the door, then back to Sheila.

'I think it might be better if you went out by the conservatory.' There was no pretence at covering up the fact that
she wanted to see the back of Sheila and, more important,
didn't want her to collide with whoever had been riding the
motorcycle.

But she was too late.

'Well, well, little Mother. Visitors! An improvement! I
thought it might have been one of your boyfriends.'

A young man in black leather gear appraised Sheila
frankly, apparently mentally undressing her from top to toe
and nodding approval. He was handsome in a weak way,
unmistakably his mother's son with her vivid eyes, but the
jaw was slack and there was a loose, uncoordinated air
about him. He had the look of a man out of control who
enjoyed the jolting effect he had on other people.

'Miss Tracy was just leaving, Nicholas.' Eleanor Rushton's attempt to retrieve some dignity from the ugly intrusion
carried no weight with her son.

'You're the one who's been causing a hassle about Harry
Riley, aren't you? Poor old Harry! Sacrificial lamb.' He
weaved awkwardly towards Sheila. She had the curious
feeling he was silently observing her but in an entirely
different context, like a stranger, claiming an acquaintance
you can't recall.

'Nicholas! You've . . .' Eleanor Rushton bit back whatever she was about to say but he finished it for her.

'Drinking. Yes, Mother. I have been drinking. That's a crime, Miss . . . Sheila Tracey. The noted lady reporter for the *Seahaven Telegraph*, the propaganda sheet for our great and glorious and good and decent town. Daughter of our lately beloved and respected bank manager!' He waved his arms mockingly above his head, causing him to stumble against Sheila.

'Nicholas!'

'Nice,' he murmured, feeling Sheila's shoulders as he drew himself more or less erect. 'Mother, Miss Tracy, doesn't approve of my drinking. The fact is, Miss Tracy, I'll let you into a little secret, Mother doesn't approve of *me*. Not that she'd admit it. Not for publication, you understand.' The words came out slurred, despite his effort to articulate them clearly.

'You must forgive Nicholas, Miss Tracy. You know what young men are when they've had a night out.' Mrs Rushton tried to make it sound as if her son were guilty of nothing more heinous than a hangover, but there was a steely undertone to her excuse for him.

'A night out!' He echoed her words with elaborate gratitude. 'What a nice way you have of putting it, Mother. Mother always finds a nice way of putting things. Have you noticed that yet, Miss Tracy?' He stared stupidly at her as if actually expecting an answer to his question.

Sheila almost felt sorry for Eleanor Rushton. Whatever the circumstances that had shaped Nicholas, it couldn't be easy acknowledging him as her son.

She forced a smile. 'I think your mother's right and you should sleep it off. In any case, I really was just leaving . . .'

'Oh, not yet, Miss Tracy. Or may I call you Sheila? Sheila.' He rolled her name round his tongue. 'We've so much to talk about.'

'Not now, Nicholas. Another time.'

'Maybe there won't be another time, Mother dear.' He looked over Sheila's shoulder at Eleanor Rushton with a

sober coldness that was more menacing than his display of
drunken arrogance.

She felt an overwhelming need to escape from this deadly
exchange between mother and son. Hastily, she said her
goodbyes.

As Eleanor Rushton opened the front door for her, she
drew Sheila aside and whispered. 'You mustn't pay any
attention to Nicholas when he's like this. It's . . . it's a
disease. He doesn't know what he's saying.'

All the same, thought Sheila, when the door was abruptly
closed behind her, I'd like to be a fly on the wall when they
really get going. Nicholas Rushton may be an alcoholic, but
it wasn't the only disease he was suffering from. She was
sure of that.

CHAPTER 15

The sound of raised voices from the morning-room followed
Sheila as she started to walk down the long, winding
drive. The powerful motorbike was clumsily parked half
across the paving, its nose mown into a bed of dahlias,
nipping the sturdy plants in the bud. She was about to
skirt around it when she stopped in her tracks. Listening.
Only the angry voices pierced the lazy calm of a Sunday
morning.

The morning-room window, she'd noticed, faced on to a
small arbour reached by a path that detoured off the main
drive. It was fringed with shrubs and hidden from the rest
of the house and the road. Swallowing a natural revulsion
against what she was about to do, Sheila picked her way
carefully through the path and knelt behind a protective
rhododendron bush beneath the open window. She held her
breath, fearing that the two people inside might have heard
her. But there was no pause in the torrent of abuse. The

wounding words battered back and forth like bullets seeking a target.

Aware of how ridiculous she must look as she crouched on the moist earth, she consoled herself for being a peeping Tom with the thought that there was a first time for everything and that it might even be in a good cause.

'How can you humiliate me like that.' The shrill tone was Eleanor Rushton's although it's doubtful whether many of the people in Seahaven who knew her would have recognized it.

'Humiliate you! That's a good one. You've done a fair job of humiliating yourself all these years. Except you don't even recognize the damage you've done. It's all show, put on an act. So long as you fool enough people with that oh so lovely image, you don't care. Well, you've fooled me once too often.'

'I don't even know what you're talking about.' There was a note of desperation in her voice.

'Don't you, don't you honestly, Mother dear?' There was no slur in Nicholas's speech now. The biting words came out clear and precise, meant to inflict the maximum hurt.

For a moment there was silence and Sheila caught her breath again, wondering whether they'd noticed they were being overheard. From her cramped position she couldn't see them.

But the silence was broken. 'Nick, I know we've never been able to get on. You've never talked, confided in me. But why, why—this?' She was speaking more rationally now.

'Oh no, you're not going to get me that way. It might work with your slaves and admirers. But not with me. I know you too well.'

'I've tried, God knows I've tried with you. There's a rotten streak. If it hadn't been for you, Sarah . . .'

'So we're back to that again. If only I'd seen her home that night. If Nick's naughty you can always call him to heel by bringing that up. Well, I've paid for that night. And I've got to live with it.' There was a break in his voice, the rage giving way to anguish.

'Nick, Nick, why won't you tell me?' She was speaking so softly now that Sheila could barely catch her words. But her attempt at reconciliation was bitterly repulsed.

'You're a marvel, Mother. You live in a world of let's pretend. If you ignore what you don't want to remember, you can convince yourself it never happened. Well, I'm past caring. Go on pretending. You can trust poor, drunken Nick not to spoil the illusion.'

'Have you finished?' Eleanor Rushton had regained the cool composure Sheila had so recently witnessed. She imagined that implacable face and shuddered in sympathy for her son. 'If you go on like this I'll have to have you committed as an alcoholic!'

Her son laughed sourly. 'A nice drying-out period. I'm sure Dr Bile could arrange that. That would suit your book nicely, wouldn't it?'

'You leave me no choice.'

The voices became fainter and then a door banged. A moment later Sheila heard a click as if a telephone had been taken off its cradle. She was conscious of a sudden, sharp pain in her right leg which was crunched underneath her. As she tried to ease the cramp a shadow blocked out the sunlight and there was a crackle of leaves behind her.

'Looking for something, miss?'

She turned round quickly. She noticed first the large spade, then the man who was holding it, hefty and weather-beaten. He was wearing a heavy duty sweater, with corduroy trousers tucked into wellington boots. She cursed herself for not remembering Yates, the gardener, although it hardly seemed likely he'd be working on a Sunday. He had more the unmistakable look of a bodyguard.

She hadn't wished so heartily for the good earth to open up and swallow her since she'd fallen flat on her face centre-stage at a school speech day. To cover her confusion she grappled around on the ground. 'My ear-ring. I think I may have lost it,' she volunteered, horribly aware that it was an absurdly lame excuse for being caught crouching under an open window at Oakley Hall. 'I've been visiting Mrs Rushton and I thought I might have dropped it around here.'

The man looked pointedly at her ears. Both pearl ear-rings she'd clipped in that morning were firmly in place. She touched them and attempted to laugh. 'Silly,' she said, plucking one lobe. 'This one is loose. I thought . . .' Her words petered out. It was an irretrievable situation and the best she could do was to beat a hasty retreat.

He helped her to her feet. 'You've dirtied your nice skirt, miss.' As she stumbled down the drive, she looked back over her shoulder. Leaning on the spade, he was still watching her.

It seemed an eternity before she reached her car, fumbled with the lock and sank gratefully into the driving seat. Her mouth was dry and a raging headache was beating an infernal tom-tom just above her temples. She gripped the steering-wheel with shaking hands in an effort to control them.

'Idiot, idiot, idiot!' she muttered, while realizing she wasn't abusing herself for eavesdropping but for being found out, like the thief who wasn't sorry he stole but was awfully sorry he got caught.

Several deep breaths and a good mental talking to later, she felt steady enough not to be a hazard on the road. As she drove off, after a nervous crunching of gears, she was almost sure she spotted a metallic grey Mercedes parked discreetly in a side lane.

'I don't imagine you'll be on Eleanor Rushton's visiting list after today.' Sheila had interrupted Stephen in the middle of composing a crucial chapter in his latest science fiction saga. He hadn't appeared best pleased. In common with the poet in *Reuben, Reuben,* he'd always maintained that the most tedious thing about writing was the paperwork.

The bleak bachelor study, bare of distractions, where he closeted himself during what he laughingly called 'my hours of creation' was located in the darkest and most inhospitable part of his house. The small, high window looked out on to a paved area cluttered with garden junk. His desk on which sat a battered typewriter was surrounded by reference books and the complete works of Ray Bradbury, Issac Asimov, Arthur C. Clarke and Stephen Gough. A coffee percolator bubbled away incessantly on the top of a bookcase. The only sign of comfort in the room was a huge, sloppy armchair that had seen far better days in which Sheila was now curled up, her legs tucked tightly beneath her.

'Is that all you've got to say?' Sheila sounded aggrieved as she cupped her hands around a mug of lukewarm black coffee. Then she looked at the desk strewn with scribbled notes and the sheet of paper in the typewriter and felt immediately contrite. She'd agonized enough over a typewriter herself not to sympathize with a writer whose thoughts have been interrupted in mid drift. 'I'm sorry, Steve, I shouldn't have come. But Dad's playing golf and I just had to unwind.'

He smiled ruefully and ripped the page out of the machine. 'No, I'm the bear with the sore head. Sticky patch! Still, the nice thing about doing this job full-time is that you can always pick it up tomorrow. More coffee?'

She made a face. 'You could dye black-out curtains in it.'

'Drink, then. I have my secret supply in times of dire need.' He opened the bottom drawer of his desk, took out a bottle of Scotch, poured a tot into her mug and another into his own.

'Bottoms up!'

'Steve, it was so eerie,' she said after taking a sip. 'Watching the two of them at it hammer and tongs and then listening to that awful conversation. And even now I'm not even sure why she invited me to call. At first I thought she was sounding me out, trying to find out how much I knew. Then this absurd ploy about me helping out with the Festival. She's so . . . so intimidating. I suppose I made a bloody fool of myself.'

'Not really, from what you say. I'd probably have done exactly the same.'

'You wouldn't have been caught snooping beneath the window, though.'

'I'm not so sure. I've done worse than that in my time for a story. Are you sure you saw Jack Murray's car in the side road?'

'I couldn't swear to it. I don't imagine his is the only Mercedes in Seahaven. But after yesterday . . .' Her voice trailed away. 'What the hell was he doing in Shoreham?'

Steve unwound his body from behind the typewriter. 'Nothing sinister there. His company owns the new leisure complex.'

She sat bolt upright. 'Why didn't you tell me this before?'

'You didn't ask me. What's so peculiar about that? You know he has fingers in several property pies along the coast.'

'God, you can be thick for a bright man sometimes. That was built on the site of the burned warehouse. He got the land cheap from the original owners. That's what Esther Bailey told me, although she didn't mention Jack Murray.'

He thumped his forehead with his fist. 'I should have cottoned on to that. But it doesn't prove that he was implicated in the fire, just that he was a shrewd businessman to move in on a good deal when it arose. All the same, you're right. Too many people here seem to have been someway involved—or in Edgar Blythe's case—very carefully not involved in the case for it to be entirely coincidental.'

'That's a cautious estimate. You sound like a lawyer.'

'I think after today a little caution wouldn't come amiss, Sheila. There's something else that's been bugging me. The cashier at the Palace said Harry had been identified on the night he died because he'd been there before. There'd been some sort of punch-up between him and local tearaways.'

'I remember. At least I think I do. Or maybe I can give an educated guess at what happened. It wasn't so long before Harry died. He came into the office one morning. He'd got a black eye, a cut lip, bruises.'

'Trouble-prone little blighter, wasn't he?'

Sheila ignored the remark. 'A gang of boys had been mugging people in that area. Harry wanted to follow up the story. Alec wasn't keen.'

'Why?'

'Because of exactly what happened. It was a Brighton story, not a Seahaven one, and he figured Harry would land himself in just the trouble he did.'

'But Harry went ahead anyway?'

'You couldn't stop him when he thought he was on to something that might turn out big. You know Harry. He got all his ideas about how a reporter operates from the movies. Apparently he'd tracked the louts down to the Palace and like a fool confronted them.'

'He didn't have the sense to call in the police first? Like someone else I know.'

She ignored that barbed crack at her, too. 'Whatever you say about Harry, he delivered the goods there. The police set a trap for them and the boys were arrested two days later.

'So Harry was a hero.'

'Not really. He got a ticking off from Alec and the police for taking the law into his own hands.'

'Seems to have been a habit with him. And while we're talking about taking the law into your own hands . . .'

She uncurled herself from the armchair and stretched. 'You're about to give me another lecture, aren't you?'

He watched her, admiring the supple figure and the stubborn look on her face. 'No. I'm reminding you that you're getting deeper and deeper into something uglier perhaps than you imagine and, if you don't watch out, next time you might end up with more than egg on your face.'

'I can look after myself,' she said truculently.

He shook his head. 'You're a cussed woman.'

He was about to enlarge on the subject when the doorbell rang.

'Damn and blast! I'll get rid of them,' he said as he strode out of the room and into the hall. She heard the front door open and a whispered consultation.

She was idly tidying the papers on his desk with her back to him when he returned, although she knew he hated anyone to interfere with his notes, 'organizing my mess' as he put it. 'Did you get rid of them?'

'No,' he said finally. 'You're not going to like this, Sheila. It's Jimmy Grant. He wants to see you. It seems the mountain has come to Mohammed and high time, too.'

CHAPTER 16

'You bastard, Steve! You called him.'

'Get hold of yourself Sheila. How could I have called him? I didn't even know you were coming here.'

She glared at him angrily, nursing her grievance, while knowing it to be fragile and unfounded.

'Anyway, what are you trying to prove by not confiding in the police?' he said, carefully controlling a temper that was near to snapping. 'Is it vanity—or what? Do you think you're smarter and tougher than they are? That was Harry's trouble and look where it landed him. Besides, Grant's not even in uniform. He just wants a little talk with you.'

In his baggy Sunday tweeds, Inspector James Grant looked more like a country vet than a policeman. In his early forties, he appeared older than his years, settled and comfortable in a job that usually made more demands on his diplomacy in handling community relations than on his astuteness in apprehending hardened criminals. Seahaven suited him ideally and he suited it. But the air of genial reasonableness could be deceptive. He was still, by training and vocation, a good policeman.

From the warmth of his manner no one would have guessed that he was on official business, although he declined Steve's offer of a drink.

'Not exactly on duty, just a friendly warning,' he excused himself, fixing kindly eyes on Sheila. 'They had a complaint at the station about you, this morning. The sergeant had the sense to contact me. When I called your home I caught Andrew just as he was leaving and he told me if you weren't at Mrs Rushton's you might be here. As Mrs Rushton filed the complaint I took a chance and came by. It's not something I'd like to discuss on the telephone.'

Sheila took a deep breath and sank into an easy chair, avoiding the accusatory look on Steve's face which clearly said, 'Be sure your sins will find you out.'

'Why would Mrs Rushton complain? She invited me to call,' she said, wilfully misunderstanding Jimmy Grant. For the second time that day she wished she could subside into the woodwork.

'I don't imagine she invited you to deliberately eavesdrop on a private conversation. Her gardener, Yates, said he found you lurking in the grounds under an open window. He observed you for several minutes. Now if Yates is lying . . .'

'He wasn't lying.' Spelt out like that, it all sounded so trivial and demeaning. 'But I hardly think it warranted calling the police.'

Jimmy Grant sighed, relaxed and, uninvited, took a seat. 'Neither do I, to be honest. Maybe I will have that drink, Steve. Obviously you touched a raw nerve with Eleanor Rushton and she's trying to get back at you. I must say I was surprised. It doesn't sound like her at all. But you understand I had to follow it up. I can probably smooth it over and there'll be no need to made it official.'

'That's very . . . very magnanimous of you, Jimmy.'

He accepted a glass of sherry from Steve, took out his pipe and leaned forward confidentially, shedding the air of officialdom he'd brought with him.

'I wouldn't be so magnanimous, Sheila, if I didn't know you were heading towards some kind of trouble.'

She looked quickly at Steve, who nodded reassuringly.

'Steve showed you the warning I received the other night.'

'He did. He also told me that, for some reason I can't fathom, you didn't feel free to bring it to the attention of the police—or me, as a friend—yourself.'

'And what could you have done about it?'

'Not a lot, I grant you. Everyone in the district received those circulars. But at least I'd have been on the alert. Sheila, I've known you since you were a young girl. You've always been open and honest before. Why so secret now?'

'Harry Riley!' she said bitterly, as if just mentioning the dead boy's name explained everything, which in a way it did.

'Harry Riley died of injuries almost certainly caused by falling off a cliff possibly while under the influence of drink. The post mortem report hasn't been made public, but those are the findings. There is no evidence that he was murdered and certainly none that might suggest he committed suicide. The police aren't fools, Sheila. We don't take any death lightly. Now if you have any proof to the contrary, give it to me. If you haven't . . .'

'What about that note to me? Forget Harry Riley! What about the ruckus at the Festival committee meeting?'

'I'm afraid all that proves is that Harry Riley was disliked. I didn't like him myself. All those wild accusations he used to make about corruption, double dealings, dirty tricks. You know yourself there was no basis in most of them. I know that Jack Murray sails close to the wind in his business affairs. But what he does isn't illegal, just very sharp. I know the Blythes are members of the National Front. That's not a criminal offence—although personally I wish it were.'

'And what about Eleaner Rushton?'

'What about Eleanor Rushton? I know you've been in-quiring about her daughter, Sarah, who was raped. And the warehouse fire in which the boy who assaulted her was killed.'

'Nice going, Steve,' she said, shrugging off his calming hand on her shoulder.

'Steve did what was right. He was only trying to protect you. Now I'm going to tell you something I shouldn't and then perhaps you'll stop harassing Eleanor Rushton. Sarah isn't abroad.'

'I thought not.'

'Don't interrupt. She was always an unstable girl and she never recovered from her experience. She's in a mental institution, has been for four years now. Only a few people, including Dr Bile, know this. Mrs Rushton has every right to keep that particular skeleton—if you can call it that—to herself if she wants to. And *you've* no right to reopen old wounds. If you think you have, then I've misjudged you all these years.'

Sheila felt her body go limp. 'I'd no idea,' she whispered. 'No wonder she has such a down on her son. If he hadn't stayed at the party that night . . .'

'Don't you think her relationship with her son is her business too?' Jimmy Grant said gently. 'Nicholas is the cross she has to bear. He's always been a black sheep. If he hadn't had the connections he did, he'd probably have ended up in Borstal when he was growing up. And the fact that Harry Riley was so tied up with him was one of the reasons why I wasn't exactly enamoured of your Harry.'

'Nicholas—and Harry?' She couldn't think why but she was genuinely surprised. The two might have had some things in common, but not the vital element. Harry was an achiever, a life force, who applied himself wholeheartedly to scaling the ladder of success. Nicholas was a degenerate, a loser, she suspected, from the day he was born.

'Latterly they were thick as thieves.'

'Then it's possible Nicholas could have confided in him about something Harry needed to know. Maybe something about the warehouse fire.'

Guilty as she felt about unwittingly aggravating Eleanor Rushton's grief about her daughter, Sheila couldn't suppress a surge of excitement. The unlikely partnership of Nicholas and Harry could have only one explanation.

She was aware that Jimmy Grant was staring at her with a look of irritated resignation. 'You don't give up, do you? Do you think you're alone in knowing of Riley's interest in that case? When he first arrived in Seahaven he came to me with a lot of trumped-up reasons why Martin Bailey was wrongly convicted. I went through the motions with the Brighton police. But there wasn't a shred of hard evidence. Just suspicion and speculation. But that's by the way. I still can't understand why you, of all people, should go skating off engaging in your own little private investigations instead of coming to me.'

She laughed, a small, cynical laugh that seemed foreign to her nature. 'You've just answered your own question, Jimmy. What joy did Harry get out of going to the police? Quite dispassionately, what would your professional reaction be if a member of the public came along with a long list of unprovable suspicions and proceeded to accuse a group of upright citizens of conspiracy to murder on no evidence but—*instinct*.' She emphasized the last word, expecting to be reprimanded at most or ridiculed at least.

Surprisingly, Steve came to her defence. 'It's true, Jimmy. How many times in your cups have I heard you complain about the amount of police time and patience that has to be taken up with little old ladies who are convinced that the neighbours are guilty of God knows what because they looked at them cross-eyed over the garden fence.'

A flicker of a grudging smile crossed Jimmy Grant's tanned face. 'I don't see the connection, but I take your point. All the same, I can't believe that Sheila backed off because she was afraid of appearing foolish.'

'Only partly.' Suddenly she felt stifled by the calm reasonableness of the two men, their too rational solicitude. Yet she had no defence against it. She who had lived her life logically and methodically had no logical or methodical arguments to support her actions for the past few days. It was as if Harry had willed her his own obsession to seek out the truth and it was up to her to guard that legacy jealously. 'I know this must sound silly. But I feel I owe it to Harry.'

It was a lame explanation. Perhaps Stephen understood it. She doubted whether Jimmy Grant did.

He clapped his hands on his thighs in a gesture that plainly indicated his exasperation and stood up. 'If you want my opinion, I think you're taking this all far too seriously, creating a mystery that probably doesn't exist. I can't stop you behaving foolhardily. But, just remember, when you trespass on people's lives, on the secrets everyone's entitled to, they're not going to take too kindly to it. Harry had nothing to lose . . .'

'. . . except his life.'

'That's *your* theory. I repeat, Harry Riley had nothing to lose. But you're putting at risk the very fabric of your life in this community, making enemies of friends, or at least well-wishers, casting aspersions . . .'

'You mean I'm rocking the boat.'

'I'm thinking of you, Sheila. How do you imagine you'll live with yourself, with Seahaven, after you're finished playing your little game? Anyway, don't let me or anyone else catch you snooping around like a sneak thief again.'

He saw in her stricken face that he'd hit home. 'Cheer up. And if you **won't** listen to me, maybe you'll listen to

Steve. Anyway, I'm off. With luck I'll still get in a round of golf. I'll make up some story for Andrew. He needn't know about this.'

'You don't have to worry about my father. He's the one who told me I'd always regret it if I didn't face up to my moment of truth. He did, you know.' She looked at him earnestly.

Jimmy Grant puckered his lips but said nothing. He'd always credited Andrew Tracy with more sense than to indulge the hare-brained fantasies of a suggestible girl.

'Will I?' She turned to Steve after the Inspector had taken his leave. He knew instinctively what she meant.

'Live with yourself, Seahaven, after all this? You're tougher than you think, Sheila. But it won't be the same. You won't be the same. You'll look at people differently and you'll think about yourself differently. You'll see the familiar faces, but you'll wonder what's ticking away behind them. It won't be pleasant. Growing up never is.'

She was grateful to him for not reminding her that he'd said exactly this to her the day before in the pub after her meeting with Joe Slack, but the growing-up remark rankled.

'Have I always seemed that adolescent to you?'

His smile was full of affection for the girl she'd been and, more, for the woman she was becoming. 'Only in your trusting nature, my dear. Am I forgiven?'

'For putting Jimmy Grant in the picture? I suppose so,' she admitted.

'He could be an ally. If an ally is needed.'

They spent the rest of the day together, making a hash of a new recipe she'd seen in the *Sunday Times* colour supplement and lazily watching an old black and white movie on television in the afternoon. By mutual but unspoken consent they didn't discuss Harry Riley, Eleanor Rushton or burned-out warehouses in Shoreham.

CHAPTER 17

She was woken out of a restless sleep by the strident peal of the telephone which pierced the stillness of the night like the urgent wailing of a banshee. She lay there for a few seconds, not quite sure whether the insistent ring was a reverberating echo of her jumbled dream or part of the real world. She heard her father lumbering down the stairs. The ringing stopped and faintly through her closed door she listened to him gruffly complaining, 'Do you know what time it is?' Then there was a long silence followed by an angry whispered conversation, too muffled for her to make out what was being said.

Yawning, she pulled on her dressing-gown and went to the top of the stairs.

'I don't want you talking to her.' Andrew was speaking in the measured tone she'd heard so often when he was trying to make a point that wilfully escaped a particularly thick client.

'Dad, I'm here,' she called.

He stiffened at the sound of her voice, then cupped the mouthpiece with his hand as he turned round.

'I didn't want to waken you. It's just some clown. Sounds drunk to me. I can tell him you're dead to the world.'

'No, I'll come.' She was already half way down the stairs.

'It's just a nuisance call. Go back to sleep, Sheila.'

'Fat chance,' she said. She reached for the receiver, wrenching it out of his reluctant hand.

'Who is this?'

'Did I wake Daddy's little girl? Daddy's little girl!' The slurred voice repeated the phrase, enjoying its derisive echo. Then there was a low chuckle which carried on obscenely as if the caller were incapable of controlling it.

She raised her eyebrows at Andrew who was standing over her with a worried expression on his face. 'You're right! Smashed out of his mind,' she murmured.

'Cut him off.'

But the voice seemed to anticipate the action. 'Don't cut me off. You remember me. Wicked, naughty Nicholas. Nobody loves Nicholas.' The maudlin mumbling continued. 'Unlovable, that's me.'

'What the hell do you want?' Her exasperation must have transmitted itself through the fog of alcohol.

'I want to see you, nice lady. Nice lady Sheila. I want to see you.'

She shivered. Half of her wanted to hear what this poor, pathetic wreck of a young man had to say, while the other half shied away at the prospect. She tried to collect her thoughts. The night cast eerie shadows. By daylight this bizarre conversation could be put into some kind of perspective.

'Why don't you sleep it off' she said, more gently. 'Tomorrow. In the morning.'

'Not now, not now?' Again that idiotic repetition. 'Morning. By the birdbath.'

'Birdbath?'

'Warrior birds. Clever little things. Won the war. D'you know that? Cleverer than people. Cleverer than Harry.' He was snickering again, savouring his crazy astuteness in drawing his own incomprehensible analogy.

The incongruity of his proposed meeting-place in the public gardens seemed to her almost amusing. 'All right. Ten o'clock.'

She wondered if he'd heard or understood her.

'Warrior birds. Boom, boom!'

As he burbled on inanely, she heard the click of an extension phone being lifted, then: 'Nick!'

It was Eleanor Rushton's voice and the telephone went dead. She stared at the receiver in her hand as if it were a dying thing that had suddenly breathed its last gasp but if she waited long enough might be resuscitated.

'It was Nicholas Rushton.'

'Oh!' Andrew seemed uninterested, just annoyed. 'Bloody nerve. This time of night.'

'He didn't know what he was doing—or saying, probably.'

'Public menace, that boy. You'd best not have anything to do with him. Promise me you won't, Sheila.' He sounded more concerned than the garbled telephone call warranted.

He looked weary and drained and she realized he was no longer a young man. To allay his concern for her, she nodded. 'Don't worry, Dad.' It was a white lie, for she had every intention of keeping her date with Nicholas and the warrior birds.

But it seemed to satisfy Andrew. 'He's no good, you know. He and Harry Riley were a fine pair!'

His coupling of Nicholas Rushton and Harry Riley surprised her. 'I didn't know you felt so strongly about Harry. You hardly knew him.'

'I know enough about him.' His eyes searched the familiar sitting-room as if he were seeing it as alien territory. 'It's cold. You need your sleep. Monday tomorrow.'

'Monday today.' She slipped her arm comfortingly through his. 'Monday looms over Sunday like a big, black cloud threatening to deluge the week.' It was one of those silly sayings that had become a fixture in the vocabulary of their lives, frequently uttered when either of them had a sticky week ahead. Their shared smile eased the tension but not the memory of the strange, unexpected interruption that had provoked it.

She was roused at the more seemly hour of seven by Andrew bearing a tray with tea, digestive biscuits and an early rose in a specimen vase. It was a rare treat. Cutting a flower was to him like inflicting a personal wound: he preferred his roses growing in the garden.

'Luxury!' She rubbed her eyes still heavy with sleep. 'To what do I owe the pleasure?'

'Just thought you deserved it.' He placed the tray on her bedside table. She noticed he was dressed for outdoors.

'What gets you out this early?'

'I promised Bill Sampson I'd look over his accounts for the tax man. As a favour. You know what a mess he makes of them.' Bill Sampson was a local farmer, an old friend of Andrew's, whose head for figures was notoriously unreliable.

'Why doesn't he get a regular accountant?'

'Claims he can't afford it.' Andrew smiled, knowing the farmer wasn't so parsimonious when it came to bidding for stock or equipping his dairy. 'Anyway, it keeps the old brain ticking over.'

'Well, I hope you get a decent breakfast out of it. When will you be back?'

He looked down at her for a long moment as if he were about to say something, then thought better of it. 'I'll see you later,' he said brusquely.

As she drank her tea, nibbled a digestive biscuit and smelt the rose, she wondered why her father hadn't mentioned his visit to Bill Sampson the day before, then she dismissed the thought from her mind as memories of the freakish phone call from Nicholas Rushton came flooding back.

The town had a Monday feeling about it as she parked her car and walked towards the public gardens. Shoppers looked harassed and the narrow seaside lanes were clogged with vans making their deliveries and irritated drivers late for offices and appointments.

The skies were overcast and the little clearing by the Warrior Birds memorial in the gardens seemed dark and airless. She found herself a seat and checked her watch. It was exactly ten o'clock. But she wasn't surprised that there was as yet no sign of Nicholas Rushton. She doubted whether punctuality weighed very heavily with him, if indeed he was in any condition to remember their conversation the night before.

But when the minutes ticked away she became more and more exasperated. Imagining him nursing an almighty hangover, oblivious that she was wasting her time waiting for him, only increased her irritation. Ten-thirty. I'll give him fifteen minutes more, she decided, self-righteously reminding herself that she had a job to do even if he didn't.

'Miss Tracy!'

For a split second she wondered whether she'd misjudged him, then she realized that the baritone voice belonged to Jenny Ashley who owned the stables deep in the Sussex countryside and made a lucrative living drilling horsey students in the fine art of dressage and competitive riding.

Sheila smiled a greeting. She was a pleasant, tweedy woman who devoted herself to the care of her horses with a nun-like passion.

'I hope we'll be getting a good write-up in the *Telegraph*,' she boomed.

For an instant Sheila looked at her inquiringly. Then she remembered. The events of the last few days had completely driven out of her head the fact that she'd spent the previous Wednesday attending the bi-annual gymkhana Miss Ashley organized for hopeful riders from Sussex stables. It was a ritual event and an agreeable day out that always received a good display with pictures in the paper.

'It was such a nice occasion. As a matter of fact, we'll be putting the feature together today.' Sheila hastily made amends for her lapse of memory.

But Miss Ashley dismissed her assurance with a wave of the hand as if she had a more nagging problem to think about.

'Do you mind?' She squatted heavily beside Sheila, her Harris tweed skirt splaying out over ample hips and thighs.

'Of course not.'

'It's really quite fortuitous running into you like this. I so rarely come to town. It just happened I had to see my solicitor today.' She spoke with that slight disdain born and bred country people adopt in referring to cities. Seahaven or Soho, it was all the same to Miss Ashley. 'If I hadn't seen you I'd probably have called you. Just to put my mind at rest. I'm sure it was nothing, nothing at all. All the same it worried me a little.'

Oh God, she's going to ask me not to mention that her prize pupil took a tumble at the water jump. 'What exactly . . . ?'

'It's about that reporter of yours. What's his name? I read about it in the paper. The one who was killed falling off the cliff.'

'Harry Riley?' What on earth could Jenny Ashley have to do with Harry?

'That's him. When we were packing up he phoned the stables on Wednesday. He wanted to speak to you urgently. I told him that you'd just left and he could probably reach you at the office. But he said he was phoning from the office, so I said he should call you at home. He didn't seem at all keen, but I assured him you wouldn't mind. I hope you didn't.'

'Naturally not.'

'Well, that's all right then. I expect it wasn't anything. He sounded very frenetic. But I know newspaper people tend to be like that. I didn't mean to pry.'

'You're not prying, Miss Ashley. I'm grateful to you. Except . . . except he didn't reach me. I didn't hear from him that day.' If only I had, Harry, if only I had. Maybe! She tried to smother the speculative 'maybe', but she knew it would continue to prick her conscience. Maybe if he'd spoken to me, somehow, some way, I could have prevented the tragedy that befell him in the dark, secret hours of the night.

'How very strange. But as I said, it probably didn't mean anything. It was just seeing his name in the paper and that dreadful accident, I felt I had to tell you.' She hoisted herself from the wooden seat with the awkward gracelessness of a woman who clearly felt more at home in the saddle. 'That's taken a weight off my mind. It's amazing how silly little things niggle at you, isn't it.'

She beamed amiably at Sheila with her rosy, outdoor face, placidly at peace with herself and the rest of the world. 'It's a lovely spot, isn't it? Quite a haven! I always stroll through before I do battle with the town.' And with a cheery wave, she launched into battle.

Lucky Miss Ashley, thought Sheila. A weight off your mind, but another weight on mine.

It was nearly eleven by the time she decided that Nicholas Rushton wasn't going to keep his appointment with her. She wended her way to the *Telegraph* offices trying to fend off a feeling of impotence. She'd been no help to Harry when he was alive. And now that he was dead, it seemed, she was just as useless. But it didn't alter her conviction that somewhere there was a key to the mystery, staring her in the face. Perhaps something so obvious that she was too close to see it.

CHAPTER 18

'Exciting, isn't it?'

She'd never seen the normally sullen Daphne Walters so animated. Her cheeks were flushed and the washed-out blue eyes sparkling. Good lord, thought Sheila, she's almost pretty!

'What's exciting?'

'The police and everything. Quizzing everyone about Harry. What he did. Who his friends were. You don't suppose he was murdered, do you?'

Bully for the police, Sheila reflected, she'd underestimated them. And she felt a sudden flood of relief. Perhaps after all, her run-in with Jimmy Grant had been more productive than she'd thought. Maybe now the burden would be lifted. Maybe the law would race to the rescue, solving all the conundrums that had kept emerging, like small babushka dolls hidden inside larger dolls, during the past few days. She was grateful that Daphne didn't seem to require replies to her questions.

'Just think! I could have been the last person to see him alive.' There was an unpleasant, preening note in Daphne's voice, as if the girl was already casting herself in the role of a star witness and enjoying the mental image.

'What?'

'Well, I *might* have been.' She tossed her head irritatedly, her fantasy fading under Sheila's candid stare.

Sheila sighed. 'I suppose you are going to tell me what you're talking about.'

The girl looked a trifle miffed, then she leaned forward dramatically, lowering her voice to a whisper. She wasn't often the centre of attention and she intended relishing every moment of it.

'You know he was last seen at the cinema in Brighton.' She paused importantly, paying out her story as frugally as if it were the plot of a long-running TV series.

'Well,' she went on, 'I was going to meet him there.'

'You mean you were the date he was keeping at the Palace.' Sheila grinned. Even in her present state of mind she couldn't help but see the humour of it. The entry in Harry's diary that had seemed so sinister was merely a reminder that he was going to meet a girl at the pictures. No mysterious rendezvous with a dark stranger. Just Daphne.

'What are you laughing at? The police were very interested.'

'I'm sure they were, Daphne. I'm not laughing at you. Just at me.' And Stephen, she thought. 'You were at the Palace with Harry the night he died.'

'Well, not exactly. I mean, I didn't go, did I!' It was a

statement, not a question. The girl shrugged, visibly de-
flated. Her moment of glory was over. 'He'd been pestering
me for days to go·out with him.' Now that Harry was dead
there was no harm in embroidering her own desirability.
There was, after all, no one to refute it. 'I kept saying no.
But then when there was all the fuss about that movie I
thought I wouldn't mind seeing it. But I wouldn't want to
go alone. So I said all right, if he'd take me to see it. Mean
bastard, he told me he'd meet me inside. I mean, I don't
mind paying my way. All the same . . .'

'At eight o'clock.'

'How do you know?'

'I guessed,' said Sheila quickly.

'But then when it came to the day, Wednesday, I reminded him,' Daphne rattled on. 'He didn't seem to remember, sort of distracted, you know, as if he'd got things on his
mind. But he said OK, he'd see me there.'

'Did he·say anything else? About what was bothering
him?'

'No, just "What's the difference, it can keep, it's kept this
long." Something like that. I didn't pay much attention.'

'So, why didn't you go after all?'

'I heard from Molly Arkwright that he was supposed to
be meeting her at the disco afterwards. Well, I've got my
pride, same as anyone else. I thought: sod that for a lark.
Dumping me at the Palace and going off with someone else.
I just decided not to turn up. Well, wouldn't you?'

Sheila gravely agreed that in similar circumstances she'd
probably have done exactly the same. 'But why didn't you
say all this last week? After they found Harry.'

The girl bridled at the implied criticism. 'I didn't think.
Actually it slipped my mind. I met this terrific boy the same
day in the hamburger joint, you see.' She launched into a
glowing report on the terrific new boy who had obviously
lived up to expectations all over the weekend. Something of
a record for Daphne's boyfriends. It was easy to see how

Harry could have slipped her butterfly mind. Already he was consigned to the debris of forgotten trivia.

'Poor Harry!' Sheila hadn't realized she'd said it out loud.

Daphne looked up sharply at the interruption in her flow of romantic confidences. 'If you ask me he got what he deserved.' Then the full import of what she'd just said sank in and she added apologetically, 'I didn't mean *that* exactly. But he wasn't *liked*, was he? Anyway, he probably had company at the Palace,' she said brightly as if the thought had just occurred to her.

'How do you mean?'

'Some chap phoned for him, just as I was leaving. He wasn't here and I told him I knew Harry was going to the Palace.' She smiled snidely, recalling this final flourish to her act of putting Harry in his place.

'Did he identify himself? Give a name?'

'No.'

'But you did tell the police that?'

The girl affected an exaggerated interest in the mauve varnish on her fingernails. 'Well, it . . .'

'I know. It slipped your mind.'

There was one thing you could say for Daphne, Sheila reflected, as she pushed her way through the swinging door to the editorial offices, you could always rely on her unreliability.

She wondered briefly who had called Harry on the evening before he met his death, whether it was the man with the good shoes and nice hands that had so impressed the cashier at the Palace. But it was a futile exercise. She'd probably never know and the bustle of the office, aggravated by the inquiries of Jimmy Grant's men, claimed her attention.

Alec Hutchinson was leafing through the pile of readers' letters which inevitably arrived on Monday morning. The range of issues that incensed, pleased or puzzled the residents of Seahaven was a source of constant amusement and amazement to him.

'Look at this one!' he said with dry humour as Sheila came in. 'Wood pigeons! "These nasty feathered friends are fast becoming a menace of plague proportions. And some foolish people actually feed them! The Council should do something about it,"' he quoted. 'I don't know what she thinks the Council can do about wood pigeons. Still, we'll run it. Get a nice little argument going with the wild bird protection society. I hear you've been stirring it up.' There was no change in his tone and for a moment Sheila thought he was accusing her of taking sides in the wood pigeon controversy.

She looked at him blankly.

'Men in blue uniforms asking questions,' he prodded her.

'Oh!' She couldn't be sure whether he was angry or merely curious about the turn of events. But then you never could with Alec.

'Don't look so distressed. It was inevitable, I suppose. The police have to go through the motions before the inquest.'

'What do you mean—I've been stirring it up?'

'Jimmy Grant dropped the odd word or two.'

'What sort of questions were they asking?'

'The usual. Did Harry have any enemies? What were his interests? That sort of thing. His landlady gave them an earful, I gather. Most of it hearsay and gossip. They went through his desk and seemed surprised he hadn't kept a diary or a book of appointments. I always thought he did. Funny if it went missing.'

He stared steadily at her with that wry smile playing round his lips. She flushed guiltily. She supposed she should have turned over Harry's notebook to the police. And if she did now, she wondered if it would make her an accessory to something or other. Maybe concealing evidence. But it all seemed strangely unimportant. So much had happened since she'd discovered it under the 'X' obituary file. Was it really only last Friday? A mere two days ago.

'I'd give a good deal to know what you're thinking right

now, Sheila. But I don't imagine you'll tell me,' he said. 'Anyway I told Grant the paper would see to the funeral expenses when they release the body.'

'That's considerate.'

'Do I detect a note of cynicism? I'm not as insensitive as all that, Sheila.' She was surprised by the quiet compassion in his voice. 'You think you're the only one who gave a damn about Harry, don't you?' Would it surprise you to learn that I knew all along about his relationship with Martin Bailey? Why do you think I was so lenient with him, turning a blind eye to those padded expenses? I knew he'd got this obsession about proving Bailey innocent, that he was helping support Bailey's wife and child.'

She felt a sharp, sinking pain in the pit of her stomach as if he'd just dealt a low blow to her solar plexus. 'I'd no idea,' she said. How blind could she have been not to realize that Alec, of all people, would make it his business to know something about the background of his staff, especially one with such dubious credentials as Harry.

'Did Harry tell you or did you just find out?'

'Does it matter?'

His lightly bantering tone restored the conversation to a normality she could cope with.

'Why didn't you ever say anything?'

'It was none of my business. Or anyone's—except Harry's.'

'And yet you still persist in believing his death was an accident?'

'I leave that to the police. Just as you should.'

'And my outburst the other evening at the committee meeting. You just let me get on with it. And all the time you knew what Harry had been up to. I don't know whether you're a swine or a . . .'

'Saint! Spare me, please. Either way.' He cuffed her gently under the chin with his fist and picked up the file of letters. 'There's still a paper to be got out this week,' he said, consciously closing the subject of Harry Riley for the time being. 'By the way, would you mind terribly covering the Gilbert and Sullivan society's *Pinafore* tonight? Congregational church hall. Fred was going to review it and we can't let them down.'

She nodded. An evening of Gilbert and Sullivan would be pleasant. And the society's productions, if not D'Oyly Carte standard, were usually enjoyable. But the prospect was soured by his mention of Fred Happer. Again, she had that feeling of guilt. It was Fred who had started her off on this whole crazy enterprise, trying to solve the riddle of Harry's death. And she hadn't given him a serious thought since she'd left the hospital.

Alec caught her train of thought. 'I phoned the hospital. He's comfortable, but it'll take a while. Lots of rest and with luck he won't have to have a bypass operation. I doubt whether he'll be coming back to the paper. Not if Mrs Happer has anything to say about it.'

'I know,' said Sheila, recalling her bruising encounter with the lady. 'She doesn't think too highly of the newspaper profession.'

'I don't suppose you want to tell me what went on between you and Fred when you visited him?' He studied her face for a moment or two, then shrugged. 'No, I don't suppose you do.'

'There's not much you don't know, is there?'

She was about to apologize for underestimating him or something equally inadequate but he was already thumbing through the letters as if nothing of importance had taken place between them. How can he switch on and off so effortlessly, she thought, watching him chuckle to himself at some reader's prize idiocy and frowning when another raised an interesting point.

'Good old Edgar, you can always guarantee he'll come up with a peach.'

He handed her the sheet of expensive notepaper with its

embossed address. It proclaimed to the editor of the *Seahaven Telegraph* that he and his wife were appalled to learn that the town's local cinema was advertising a future screening of a notoriously disgusting film called *Punk Lust*. Not, of course, that he or Mrs Blythe had demeaned themselves to actually view such filth, but for the sake of the town's morals and the protection of its young he intended to mount a campaign to have the movie banned. A snide postscript added that 'while Brighton may be used to this sort of thing, it couldn't be supported in Seahaven.'

'It must have taken an effort of will for him not to describe Brighton as a den of iniquity,' Alec laughed. 'No wonder he moved his practice to Seahaven.'

'Will you publish it?' Sheila smiled. 'Pompous ass!' It was like a second surname. Edgar Blythe Pompous Ass. But even as she said it she wondered whether there was more to the solicitor's outrage than an exaggerated sense of morality.

'Why not? The cinema manager will probably weigh in with an argument and a few fringe lunatics will keep it going. *Punk Lust*! Doesn't he realize it's all publicity hype? It's the silliest, least sexy movie I've ever seen. Anyone who could be corrupted by that isn't safe running around loose in the real world.'

He passed the letter over to the 'in' file, apparently dismissing it from his mind. What a cool one you are, thought Sheila. For the second time that morning he'd rocked the carefully constructed image she had of him. She couldn't believe it was just a slip of the tongue.

'You mean you've actually seen the film?'

As soon as it was out she wished she hadn't said it. He turned round abruptly, knocking the letters to the floor.

'Damn!' He knelt down, picking them up and pain-stakingly filing them back in order. 'I thought I should take a look at it, when I heard it might be coming to Seahaven. I knew it would cause a bit of ruckus.'

She admired the way he cleverly diverted the attention

from himself to his role as editor of the local newspaper. Good shoes, nice hands! They fitted another role, too: the cashier's memory of the man who went to the Palace the same night as Harry.

Suddenly she wanted to back away, to be alone with her own thoughts. But before she could leave the phone rang. 'Don't leave,' said Alec over his shoulder as he picked it up.

His voice sounded uncharacteristically agitated.

'Who? Put him on.' As he concentrated on whatever the caller was saying, she watched the colour drain out of his face. When he put the phone down he looked at her silently, then seemed to recover himself.

'That was Jimmy Grant. It's Nicholas Rushton. He's dead. Motorcycle skidded into a tree on the way into Seahaven.'

Sheila closed her eyes, conscious of a sinking sensation. She steadied herself with rigid hands against Alec's desk. All the time she'd been cursing Nicholas for not turning up to meet her, he'd been lying dead by the roadside.

'It was an accident,' she said eagerly, willing it to be so.

'Seems not. A hit and run case. Car drove him off the road, early this morning. Grant said he'd let us know when he has more information. Call in Roy, would you? We'd better get someone on to it.' But he spoke as if obeying a kind of reflex action that had nothing to do with him.

He sagged into the swivel chair behind his desk, his eyes glazed. 'Oh Eleanor!' he whispered softly to himself.

CHAPTER 19

'Can I speak to Mr Tracy?' Her mouth was dry and the words came out haltingly.

'Say again!' The woman sounded cross as if she'd like to have told Sheila she couldn't be bothered with petty inquiries on a busy Monday morning and only common politeness prevented her from doing so.

Sheila repeated the request, more firmly this time.

'Hang on. I don't think he's here.'

She didn't know why her first reaction to the news of Nicholas Rushton's death had been to call her father at Bill Sampson's farm. She could have explained it in ordinary circumstances, in that blessed, complacent past that seemed so far away where there were no secrets and nothing to hide. But now even her relationship with her father had subtly changed, become more wary and guarded. What she felt was beyond logic, a prickle of irrational fear that could only be allayed by Andrew. It wasn't a physical fear. She could have dealt with that. It was as if something strange and sinister that had lain dormant in her subconscious had suddenly sprung to life demanding she pay attention.

The seconds grew into minutes, ticking away mercilessly, each one fuelling that imaginary fear. Oh God, let him be there, she repeated silently to herself, let him be there. She tried not to remind herself that the road on which Nicholas Rushton met his Maker was in the opposite direction to Bill Sampson's farm: that would have been an admission of a suspicion she couldn't countenance.

'Sheila!'

For a moment she couldn't speak, conscious only of an overwhelming sense of relief mixed with embarrassment at her own foolish doubts.

'It is Sheila, isn't it?'

'Of course, Dad. Sorry if you were in the middle of something.' The words came out in a rush, not quite making sense. Of course he was in the middle of something. Bill Sampson's accounts, just as he'd said he would be.

'Are you all right?'

'No . . . yes . . . I mean, yes, I'm all right.'

'Bill's been showing me his new heifer. That's why I took so long.'

'Mrs Sampson didn't seem to think you were around.'

'She probably thought I'd left.' He sounded surprised that she should be so interested in his movements. 'What's so important?'

'I wondered if you'd heard. About Nicholas Rushton.'

'What about him? You didn't go to see him after all?' His voice was carefully noncommittal. She cursed herself for noticing it, for reading too much into a simple question. Damn the telephone!

'He's been killed in an accident on his motorcycle. Hit and run driver.'

There was a long pause before he came back. 'It'll be a shock for Eleanor Rushton. But I suppose it was just a matter of time. The way he rode that thing and the way he drank.' He pulled himself up, seemingly aware of the callousness of his response. 'Of course, it's very sad. A young life.'

This isn't my father talking, she thought, the kind, sensitive man she'd known all her life.

As if she'd telegraphed her feelings over that impersonal telephone line, his voice returned with all the old warmth and concern. 'Don't let it upset you, Sheila. I know how you must feel, speaking to him so recently. It's a shaker, not easy to take in. But these things happen. We'll talk about it tonight.'

'Late, I'm afraid. I promised Alec I'd cover the *HMS Pinafore* production. Fred was going, but . . . Oh dad, Fred, Harry, now Nicholas. Is there any end to it?'

'There's always an end to it, Sheila, somewhere along the line.' He seemed to be convincing himself as much as he was reassuring her. 'I worry about you. I know, we'll take an early holiday this year. Maybe go abroad.'

She laughed, despite herself. 'You! Abroad! You hate abroad.'

'I'll force myself. Unless you'd rather go with Steve. It would be a good thing for you to get away for a bit.'

'Not until I've finished what I started out to do, one way or another.'

Out of the corner of her eye she saw Alec come into the now busy office. 'I have to go, Dad.'

'I know.'

She was about to put down the phone, then stopped. 'By the way, did Harry call me sometime on the day . . . last Wednesday?' She couldn't bring herself to say 'on the day he died'. Not any more.

He took an unconscionable time to reply, presumably trying to remember. 'Not that I recall,' he said finally. 'Why?'

'Nothing. Just that apparently he'd been trying to reach me.'

'Well, if I didn't put it down on the pad, he didn't. I'm a very good part-time secretary,' he joked.

'I know you are. It probably wasn't anything.' Alec was signalling her behind Roy Kennedy, who was briefing a reporter on how to cover the Nicholas Rushton story. 'Must go.'

The grave look on Alec's face drove all thoughts of Harry Riley's attempt to contact her out of her mind.

'What is it, Alec?'

He motioned her into his office away from the central editorial department.

'The police are interviewing George.' He sounded bewildered, as if not quite comprehending what he was saying.

'George Lacey? What about?' But from Alec's expression she knew she didn't need to be told.

'It was his car that drove Nick Rushton off the road.'

'How do they know?'

'The fool took it into a nearby garage with a crumpled bonnet. Not far from where they found Nick. The mechanic didn't think anything of it until he heard about the accident and then he got suspicious. Public-spirited sort, he tipped off the police. Apparently a bit bolshie about chaps who swan around in new Mercedes and wreck them. There were traces of the same paint from the motorcycle on the bonnet. I have to get down to the station. Jimmy Grant's just called me. George is in a right mess. Edgar Blythe's with him. But he'll need a good lawyer to get him out of this.'

She'd stopped listening long before he finished. 'Mercedes! I didn't know George drove a Mercedes.'

'That's the hell of it. He didn't until a couple of weeks ago. He traded in his old Rover. Jack Murray knew a dealer and got him the Mercedes at discount.'

A mental image of the grey Mercedes parked in the side road near Eleanor Rushton's house flashed across Sheila's mind. That and Lacey's bitter remark about Harry's meddling on the day after his body had been discovered at the bottom of the cliff an eternity ago.

'I should have thought the hell of it would be the loss of a young man's life,' she said coldly.

Alec threw up his hands. 'I know. I know. That was selfish of me,' he said with a decent show of remorse. 'It's just that he's my friend. And there's the business. It doesn't look good. Poor old George. Licence revoked. Maybe prison. Thank God, he hadn't been drinking. The chances are Nicholas had been. That may be George's salvation.' Already his mind was ticking over the permutations of George Lacey's possible defence. 'I hope Eleanor doesn't get to hear yet.'

'Maybe it won't come as that much of a surprise to her,' she said.

He glanced up at her sharply and his grim searching expression spanned the uncomfortable silence that lay, leaden with unspoken meaning, between them.

The overcast skies had lifted. But the sun brought with it an unsociable stiff breeze that whipped round the wooden slats of the shelter on the promenade in which Sheila huddled, shivering at each draught of chill wind.

Anyone seeing her would have thought she was merely absorbed in watching the bird lady: the diminutive ruddy-faced woman who every day could be found on the front, feeding the seagulls that swooped on her eagerly, squawking their welcome. Indeed, the ritual of the little woman, chattering to the greedy gulls as she scattered the bread from her shopping-bag on to the promenade, was curiously soothing, freeing Sheila's mind to wander.

Passers-by muttered crossly and scattered as the birds dived perilously low, skimming their heads. But the woman remained unperturbed. Occasionally a complaint brought a policeman on the scene who amiably moved her on with a caution. But the next day she would be back with her bread and her shopping-bag. She was a fixture as sturdy and unbudgeable as the statue in the town square of the bearded Victorian worthy who had laid the cornerstone of the grandiose railway station and pronounced Seahaven 'a ripping little place'.

The statue had long survived the railway station which was now derelict, a forlorn victim of Dr Beeching's programme for streamlining the British rail network in the 1960s.

The woman seemed impervious to cold or heat. Winter or summer, she always wore the same cotton print frock and bulky Shetland wool cardigan. Or perhaps she had a whole wardrobe of similar print frocks and Shetland cardigans. No one apparently knew where she lived or whence she came. Perhaps no one had bothered to inquire. She was just there, every day, around lunch-time, somehow reassuring in the certainty of her presence.

Since she was a child Sheila had been fascinated by her. Once she'd tried to speak to her, but the woman had simply smiled and stayed silent, but for her gentle wooing of the gulls.

Observing her placidly dispensing her largesse amid the curling flock of birds, Sheila envied her her apparent contentment. She huddled deeper into her jacket, feeling the cold in her bones, although it wasn't really all that bitter.

As Stephen Gough approached, he thought how small and vulnerable she looked, hunched up in a corner of the shelter.

'You could have picked a cheerier place to meet,' he said, trying to sound jovial. 'You look perished.'

She didn't look up, but the sense of his nearness seemed to relax her tensed body. 'How old do you think she is?' She nodded in the direction of the bird lady. 'I've often wondered. When I was little I thought she was a witch. A good witch. Not quite mortal.'

He sat down beside her and took her hand, cupping her icy fingers in his warm palm. He didn't say anything, waiting for her to speak.

Finally she turned towards him. 'At least now I know what I have to do. Find that item Harry discovered in the *Telegraph* files.'

He was alarmed by the expression in her eyes. It was more than determination. It was the kind of obsession he'd seen in the eyes of men whose inner turmoil had taken them beyond reason.

'What brought this on?' he asked mildly. But he already knew. It had all piled up too quickly for her. Nicholas Rushton's accident, George Lacey's involvement. And something else he couldn't quite fathom but fearfully suspected.

'Do you know what you're looking for?' he continued, when she didn't reply.

The bird lady had emptied the last crumbs from her shopping-bag. 'Away, away!' she called softly to the gulls, who shrieked their frustration and took flight over the pebbled beach and lapping waves, merging with the dappled sunlight. Then she trotted off to who knew where. Sheila watched her until she was out of sight.

'Sheila!'

She sighed. 'I heard you, Steve. Don't worry. I'm not losing my mind, if that's what you think. Do I know what I'm looking for? I believe so. The identity of the man Eleanor Rushton's been at such pains to keep a secret all these years. Her daughter's father.'

'And would that solve everything?'

'I think so. I know so. The warehouse fire. Billy Stride, Harry, maybe Nicholas. It was staring me in the face, Steve, and I couldn't really see it. Revenge. At least, originally it was revenge. Harry just got caught in the crossfire. You're not giving me an argument?'

He put his arm around her. 'Probably because I've arrived at the same conclusion myself. But I still don't like the idea of you . . .'

'Steve, I have to do this. There's no danger. Just thumbing through a lot of dusty files. Don't you see? No one's going to do it but me. No one's going to believe it. The man's alive. I feel it. He set up Martin Bailey to cover up the killing of Billy Stride. Then he murdered Harry because Harry found out who he was.

'It could be a total stranger.'

'No. He's not. That's the hell of it. George Lacey, Jack Murray, even Alec—he let slip he'd seen the movie playing at the Palace the night Harry died.'

'Don't cast me as Eleanor Rushton's mysterious lover. I was just a cub reporter on the *Daily Mirror* twenty years ago.' She looked so desperately serious he tried to make light of it.

'Don't joke, Steve.'

'I wish it were a joke. Not me, I mean. The rest of it. I suppose I can't budge you?'

She shook her head.

'All right. Look up those files. But while you're combing

through the secrets of Seahaven's past, at least I can have a word with Jimmy Grant.'

'It won't do any good. Not without evidence. He told us that.'

'Hold on. You haven't heard me out. Last Wednesday night was bridge night. Grant's a regular and so are other people on your hit list. But whoever followed Harry to the Palace and then murdered him couldn't have been playing bridge at the same time.'

For the first time since he'd seen her that morning she smiled. 'What a genius you are.'

'Not really. Just practical deduction. So why don't you hold off until I've seen him. He's not a fool, you know. And I'd feel a lot happier about you.'

'No, Steve. I've made up my mind. Nothing much is going on at the office now. It's lunch-time. The ideal time. No one will notice me burrowing around in the basement. And besides, what can happen to me? When I come up with something I'll get in touch. And then . . .'

'Then what?'

'I'll have done all I can. The law can take over. Why are you looking at me so strangely?'

'I was just thinking there are worse things than murder.'

'What an odd thing to say. What could be worse than murder?'

'I'm not sure. But I hope you never find out.' He looked at her steadily, anxiously, feeling a deep concern not for her safety, but for her sanity.

CHAPTER 20

As Sheila looked around the dingy basement she realized her brave show of certainty that the solution to the mystery of Harry Riley's death lay somewhere in the bound copies of the *Seahaven Telegraph* was a sham. Piled in racks around the walls, the dung-coloured volumes, thick with dust as the cleaning lady could only be prevailed upon to venture into the basement under threat of dismissal, seemed to have closed ranks in presenting her with an insurmountable challenge. The years, embossed in faded gold on the spines, marched in front of her, guarding their secrets jealously.

For the first time she faced the enormity of the task she'd set herself. Not only was she unsure of precisely what she was looking for, she had no idea where to look for it. If only Harry had left a clue. If only Fred Happer had noticed which volume had contained the information that had so excited him.

'But they didn't, so it's up to you, my girl' she muttered grimly. At least she could start with the reports on the warehouse fire in Shoreham and the subsequent trial. She hauled down the appropriate year in a cloud of dust, opened the volume on the table in the centre of the basement and set to work.

An hour later she leaned her back against the slat of the folding chair on which she was sitting. The muscles in her shoulders ached with weariness. But the physical discomfort was less exhausting than the mental disappointment as she realized she was getting nowhere. The reports of the fire and trial had yielded nothing she didn't already know. Then she'd selected files at random, reaching far back over the years, hoping to find some lead worth pursuing. But that, too, had proved fruitless.

Maybe, after all, she was on a fool's errand. Maybe Harry had found nothing and had simply taken the opportunity to needle Fred who had always had it in for him. It seemed more and more likely.

She surveyed the volumes heaped on the table in front of her reproachfully and massaged the back of her neck with tense fingers. While hating to admit it, she knew she was beaten. She turned her face gratefully towards the shaft of

sunlight that filtered through the high grilled window at
street level. It shot past her and settled on an undisturbed
volume at the far end of the shelves. She looked at it idly
and then with increasing interest. It had been pulled slightly
out of alignment with the serried ranks of other bound
copies, its spine an inch or two in front of them. But, more
important, there was no film of dust on it. Someone had
taken it down and wiped it clean within the past few days.

Eagerly she lugged it down off the shelf and frowned,
puzzled, as she noted the year. The volume contained copies
of the first six months of the *Seahaven Telegraph* for 1966.
There was no doubt in her mind that Harry had been the
someone who had perused it so recently, but she couldn't
imagine what could have happened in 1966 to engage his
attention or have any connection with his investigations.
Unless . . .'

She flicked over the fragile pages, yellowing at the edges.
Nothing much had changed in Seahaven over twenty years.
The same local events. The same reports of council de-
cisions, Women's Institute meetings, the same debate about
the annual festival, even the same discussions about the
dangers of the cliff road after a six-year-old boy was rescued
from certain death by a passer-by. Only the fashions had
changed. Seahaven was as comfortable and complacent in
1966 as it appeared to be in 1985.

The months passed by in receding order under her fingers.
Where, Harry, where? By the time she'd reached back to
the first week in January, she'd almost given up hope again.

The centre pages were devoted to photographs of the New
Year ball at the White Hart hotel. She scanned them quickly.
Some faces she recognized. Others had since departed. Then
one in particular caught her eye. The caption—'Seahaven
revellers toasting the New Year—' was lightly underlined
in ballpoint ink. Harry's ballpoint? The photograph seemed
at first much like all the others. A bevy of people in evening
dress with glazed smiles on their faces and raised glasses in

their hands. But in the background, seemingly oblivious of the camera, was an unmistakable figure. A young, recently widowed Eleanor Rushton was engaged in an intimate embrace with a man. But it wasn't the chummy, party embrace of friends celebrating 'Auld Lang Syne'. Even in the blurred photograph there was a passion about it that indicated a far more intense relationship. Almost fearing what she might discover, Sheila focused her attention on the man. She peered closely at him, then turned away quickly burying her head in her hands.

Waves of nausea engulfed her and she had to stifle an urge to vomit. She stayed rigid in the chair for several minutes, breathing deeply until she felt herself under control. Then she tore out the page, stuffed it in her pocket and meticulously returned the bound copies to the shelves.

She knew what she had to do.

Inspector James Grant was not best pleased when Stephen Gough put in an appearance at the station. The trouble with policing a small town was that infringements of the law occasionally involved old and good friends. He didn't relish having to charge George Lacey with dangerous driving and possibly manslaughter. Even less did he enjoy the prospect of telling Eleanor Rushton that Lacey had been responsible for the death of her son.

'I hope this is important, Steve. I'm up to my eyes,' he said testily.

'It's important.'

Jimmy Grant noted the urgency in his voice and nodded. Stephen Gough wasn't the sort of man who would waste his own or anybody else's time unnecessarily.

'What's on your mind?' he conceded grudgingly. 'If you're going to nobble me about George Lacey, save your breath. I've just had Alec Hutchinson in here leaning on my loyalty as a friend. I told him what I'm about to tell you. Lacey's admitted he was driving the Merc that collided with

Nicholas Rushton's motorcycle. That's a fact and now it's up to the lawyers and magistrates. Any mitigating circumstances about needing to get to London in a hurry to keep an appointment with some suppliers are for them to argue about. It's out of my hands.'

Stephen could sense the Inspector's well-contained outrage that his integrity as a policeman should be challenged on the grounds of old acquaintance. All the same, he was grateful that Jimmy Grant had unknowingly answered one question he now didn't need to ask. So, Lacey was simply going to London on business. No ulterior motive there.

'That's not what I want to talk about.'

Jimmy Grant observed him keenly for a moment, then brusquely ushered him into an ante-room.

'Five minutes,' he said, pointedly looking at his watch, leaving Stephen in no doubt that five minutes was all he was going to get.

'How long have you known Eleanor Rushton?'

Clearly Grant hadn't anticipated the question. 'Ten, eleven years. Ever since I transferred to Seahaven. Why do you ask?'

'Then you don't know much about her past life.'

The Inspector raised his eyebrows. 'If this is leading up to another of Sheila's cockeyed fantasies . . .'

'Wait, Jimmy. Maybe they aren't so cockeyed.'

Swiftly he gave Jimmy Grant a run-down on his conversation with Sheila that morning, filling him in on the facts that led up to it and his own fear for her safety. As he talked he could feel the Inspector's impatience giving way to interest and finally concern.

'It's supposition,' Jimmy Grant said finally.

'Isn't that where most investigations start?'

'It's a pity she wasn't as open with me as you've been.'

'She didn't feel you'd be any more receptive to her suspicions than you were to Harry Riley's. She thought you were one of them.'

'Them?'

'Seahaven.'

'What does she think the police are for?'

Stephen shrugged. 'She's been under a strain. Maybe she hasn't been quite rational. But now I think she's right. If she does come up with something in those *Telegraph* files . . . Jimmy, I'm worried.'

'All right, what do you want from me? Apart, that is from sending a man to the *Telegraph* offices and stopping her.'

'First, information. It may be nothing. But do you remember who was at the bridge night last Wednesday—or, more important, who wasn't.'

Jimmy Grant thought back to the night when Harry Riley died. Like all good bridge players, he could recall every hand he had been dealt but remembering anything else came harder. Stephen waited, hardly daring to breathe for fear of interrupting his concentration and yet dreading what he might hear.

After a while Jimmy Grant turned towards him, his eyes wide, unbelieving. 'There was one absentee. I remember now. It was a last-minute phone call. We were having a drink and . . . no, it couldn't be.'

'Jimmy, who cancelled out at the last minute? You've got to tell me.'

When he uttered the name Stephen knew his worst fears had been justified. And he also knew Sheila needed protection as she'd never needed it before and probably never would again.

'Steve, it doesn't make sense. There's never been a hint, not even a rumour. I can't believe what you're suggesting. There's no evidence.' He sounded bewildered, as if trying to square his own growing suspicion with his professional expertise as a police officer.

'Then it's time we got some evidence, before Sheila learns the truth.'

'We don't know what the truth is.'

'But Eleanor Rushton does. I think we should pay her a visit. *Now*. Before it's too late.'

'Good God, man, the woman's just lost her son.'

'I think she's traded on everyone's discretion long enough.'

Jimmy Grant seemed torn between asserting his legal authority and agreeing the sense of what Stephen was suggesting.

'All right. But I don't like it. And you keep out of it.'

'Does she know that George Lacey drove the car that killed Nicholas?'

'No. I haven't broken that to her yet. I thought I'd wait, until she'd got over the shock. He was a friend.'

'Well, do me one more favour. Don't mention it. It may be the one way of finding out what we need to know.'

Jimmy Grant shook his head wearily. 'It goes against the grain. Prying into a woman's past. I'll never forgive you for this, Steve.'

'You will,' said Stephen grimly. 'If it brings a murderer to book. Besides, I don't give a damn about Eleanor Rushton. All I care about is Sheila.'

The lock on the Victorian roll-top desk had proved surprisingly easy to pick with the help of a bent safety-pin. But if it hadn't Sheila knew where he kept the key. He'd made no secret of it.

He'd always jokingly referred to the desk as his treasure trove and there had been an unspoken understanding that it was *sacrosanct*. And he'd needed no more guarantee of privacy than the certain knowledge that she would never betray his trust. Until now.

She was amazed at how calm she felt, her hands steady, her mind clear, as if her inner turmoil had grown a protective crust. She'd left the *Telegraph* offices with an icy sense of purpose.

Only when the lock clicked and the roll-top revealed the

contents of the desk did she realize she'd no more idea what she might find than she had when she combed through the bound back copies of the *Telegraph*. But she trusted the instinct that had led her to the forbidden desk.

The papers and files were all in neat compartments. He was always very neat, she thought, almost impersonally as if he were a stranger. She didn't hurry, taking her time, as she flicked through the correspondence, receipts for paid bills, income tax returns, and returned them scrupulously to their individual drawers. Nothing there of interest. She continued her search for the best part of half an hour, working her way through to a long, narrow drawer partially hidden by a blotting-pad. It seemed immovable although it had no separate lock. But, feeling delicately down the small aperture at its side, her fingers connected with a metal catch. As she slid it forward the drawer released itself.

Inside under sheets of tissue paper was a photograph album. She drew it out carefully. She felt no shame in invading this, his secret place, only an implacable anger. The rest, the sorrow, the hurt, would come later.

She turned the pages, looking at the snapshots of her mother, herself as a child on the beach at Seahaven as if they were people she dimly recalled but had never known. On the last page but one she stared into the vividly beautiful face of Eleanor Rushton cosseting a baby who was gurgling happily into the camera. On the final page there was a photograph of a pale, mousey girl in her teens with intense, deep-set eyes. She'd seen it before on the table in the morning room at Oakley Hall. Sarah Rushton.

She was still sitting at the open desk with the album in front of her when she heard the door open behind her. She'd been too absorbed to notice the car draw up in the drive.

'What are you doing home? I thought you'd be late, Sheila.' He sounded cheerful as he always did, pleased to see her. 'I . . .' Then his voice trailed away as he took in the scene. The open roll-top desk, the album, the photograph of the teenage girl.

She turned round slowly in the swivel chair and as he faced Sheila's accusing eyes, the huge, bearlike body of Andrew Tracy slumped in the doorway. 'Dear God!' he whispered.

CHAPTER 21

At the sight of her father, his eyes filled with pain, the anger drained out of her. She was conscious only of a terrible numbness, except for that part of her brain that was urging her to run away, to hide. But her limbs wouldn't obey. She sat there motionless, staring at this man who had been the dearest person in her life, while facing the awareness that she didn't know him at all.

'Why?' she said weakly. There were so many why's to be answered, but at this moment only one seemed insupportable. 'Why did you lie to me all these years?'

He sagged limply into an armchair. It was his favourite chair, the chintz fabric a little worn with age, the cushions comforting his bulky frame. She'd watched him sitting there just like this a thousand times before. The same chair. The same man. Nothing had changed. Only everything that mattered.

'I didn't lie, Sheila. Not in so many words.' His voice seemed to come to her from a far distance, pleading for forgiveness. He leaned forward, his arms reaching towards her.

It was the familiarity of that gesture which revived her anger. How many times had she run eagerly into those arms when she'd been hurt or lonely or abused at school. How dare he think the past, the false tenor of their lives together, could be wiped out so easily!

'Don't touch me. No, you didn't need to lie. You just lived a lie.' She heard her voice rising hysterically. A voice she barely recognized. He turned away from her, unable to bear the look of revulsion that contorted her features into an ugly mask of hatred.

'Sheila! I must make you understand. You're my daughter. I love you,' he begged, willing her to believe the one decent thing they'd shared.

She watched his agony and felt nothing. The hysteria had passed, replaced by the icy composure with which she'd ransacked his desk.

'And what about your other daughter? Do you love her as much? Or more? Would you have murdered for me as you murdered for her?'

The words came out with cool precision, as if she'd rehearsed them over and over again like dialogue in a play. The great last act dénouement. This isn't me speaking, she thought. It's a character in a drama which will end when the curtain comes down. She felt herself removed, impersonal, in a cold limbo.

She observed the impact of her accusation on her father, objectively. His eyes widened under those untidy brows, heavy with grief and something more, terror.

'You don't know what you're saying,' he whispered. 'There were reasons.'

'Revenge? Is that why Billy Stride had to die, why Martin Bailey is paying for the crime you arranged, why Harry Riley was killed because he knew too much?'

'I didn't mean . . . I didn't intend . . .'

She clapped her hands over her ears. 'I don't want to hear.' But she knew she had to. It was the least, the last, respect she could pay him. Somewhere deep inside a trickle of warmth penetrated her implacable control. Compassion perhaps, not for a cheat or a murderer, but for a human being who despite everything was her own flesh and blood.

It was as if he'd sensed the relaxing of her defences. 'You

owe me this,' he urged. She took in the words but not the tone of a father desperately playing on the emotions of the daughter he knew so well. A man bargaining, if not for his life, for his peace of mind.

She sat almost dutifully staring past him, her face blank, at the curtains framing the french windows. They were frayed at the edges from constant shooshing back and forth. They'd planned to have new curtains measured but somehow had never got around to it. Odd how at this time that trivial domestic indecision was etched so clearly on her mind, an anchor on sanity. Her hands were clasped limply in her lap. She'd read about cases like this. Killers, sex maniacs who'd lived impeccable lives in the bosom of their families. When they were caught everyone who knew them intimately would have sworn on the Bible that they were the soul of kindness and respectability. She'd wondered sometimes how the relatives could have been so stupid, so unobservant, not to know they'd been leading double lives. Now she was the stupid, unobservant one. Was it because she'd been too close to him or not close enough? I'll listen, she thought, but I won't understand, I'll never understand.

Her father was talking in a monotone without passion about events that could only have been activated by passion, offering her a Renoir or a Gauguin from which all the colour had been removed.

'You have to understand how lonely I was when your mother died. Ellie—Eleanor—had been recently widowed. I fell in love with her. It's as simple as that.'

'You had me,' she said bitterly.

'It wasn't the same. You know that, Sheila. You're a woman. I wanted another kind of love. I'd hoped we might marry. But Ellie never wanted that. She enjoyed the secrecy, the hiding. I suppose I should have realized then that there was no future for us. But I kept on hoping. And then she became pregnant with—Sarah.'

'My sister. Why don't you say it?'

'I never thought of her like that. You have to believe me. I'd got used to . . . to living my life in two separate compartments. The awful thing was it wasn't hard. That's funny, it should have been. But it wasn't.'

He shook his head, puzzled, as if for the first time it had occurred to him how strangely and comfortably he'd managed to conceal that other half of his life even in the close confines of a small town like Seahaven.

'The affair ended before Sarah was born. It was Eleanor who broke it off. I still loved her.'

'And now?'

'Perhaps even now,' he admitted. 'Oh, we've always remained friendly. We've met socially. But it was over. Except Sarah was my daughter. Maybe I should have insisted on acknowledging that I was the father. But Ellie, she could always persuade me to do anything—or nothing. And one way or another I managed to see Sarah a good deal. Just as a family friend. She was never like you, Sheila.'

'I hardly knew her.' Why should she? Sarah was part of that secret life he'd so carefully kept from her.

'She was a frail little thing, helpless, vulnerable. I suppose that made me love her more. You were always so self-sufficient, cheerful, popular. You fitted in. And we did have a good relationship, didn't we? You have to grant me that.'

She closed her eyes, painfully remembering. He was right. They had had a good relationship, affectionate father, devoted daughter.

'Don't play on my sympathy. Not now,' she said brusquely, fighting back the instinct of a lifetime. 'I'm not condemning you for having an affair with Eleanor Rushton, for caring for her—your—daughter. It's the rest. How could you . . . ?' She was struck by the banality of the half-formed accusation, almost comic in its awful inadequacy. How could you burn the toast, plant the fuchsias out so early, forget to drain the tank in the outside lavatory before the first winter frost? Where were the words to express the enormity of what she was trying to say? Where was the primer that taught you the right responses to the shattering of everything you'd believed in?

He looked bewildered. Perhaps it was genuine. Perhaps it was part of the act he'd perfected over the years for her benefit. She'd never know. 'I'm not sure,' he said. 'When Sarah was raped because that wretched Nicholas couldn't be bothered to tear himself away from a party to see her home, I just felt a deep rage. Then the boy, Billy Stride, got let off so lightly and there was little Sarah in a catatonic state. Do you know what that means? It's as if her mind had atrophied. She may never recover. I went to see her often in the home for the mentally handicapped when you were away at work. She never recognized me or her mother.'

'I know when it was,' Sheila remembered. 'You were suffering from depression, the doctor said. And none of us could understand why. You had time off from the bank. I even thought it was something I'd done unknowingly.' All those weeks spent believing that somehow she'd failed him. But he didn't seem to hear her.

'That's when I decided to see that boy was punished. The law wouldn't do it. So I would. At first I just wanted to scare him. But then everything seemed to fall into place, as if I'd been granted a God-given go-ahead. Bailey came to work for Eleanor. He got very thick with Yates, the gardener. He told him all about the rumpus he'd had with Billy Stride and his pals for drug-pushing. How they hung out at the warehouse. That's how Nicholas got to hear about it and passed it on to me.'

'But why would Nicholas tell you? You hated him. You, Eleanor, blamed him—for Sarah,' she said.

He looked at her strangely. 'But don't you see, I needed Nicholas for my plan. I needed the guilt he felt about what he'd done. Although I don't think Ellie had ever told him, I knew he suspected I'd been her lover, probably that I was Sarah's father.'

'You used him, just like you used Martin Bailey,' she whispered, aghast.

'Of course. It had to be done.' He sounded so matter-of-fact and she noted the change in him. There was no remorse. His eyes were glazed, unseeing. He was talking eagerly now, mesmerized by his own confession like a man off-loading his sins on a priest in exchange for three Hail Marys and a promise not to sin again.

He was sparing her nothing: neither the calculated way he and Nicholas had monitored Bailey's movements on the day of the warehouse fire, down to stealing and planting his old rake on the site; nor the midnight break-in to Bailey's empty house when Esther was away to destroy his accounts.

'It was so easy, Sheila. No one was about. We knew those boys were in the warehouse. All it took was a couple of cans of kerosene. The place was a fire hazard anyway. It went up in flames, just like that. But I didn't think they'd die. I thought they'd get out somehow.'

'Only you never waited around long enough to find out. And when Bailey was convicted you were too cowardly to come forward.' She spoke in a small, still voice, bankrupt of emotion.

'No more cowardly than Edgar Blythe who didn't want to soil his hands with the case.'

'Can't you see the difference? Can't you *really* see the difference? And Eleanor Rushton?'

'Ellie never knew. I wanted to keep all that side of it from her and I swore Nicholas to secrecy. Unless . . .'

Suddenly, he seemed aware of Sheila's presence. Before, while he'd been talking, she'd felt as if she were merely part of his conspiracy. Now he looked at her with a new, frightening expression in his eyes, like an animal who realized he'd engineered his own trap.

'How did you find out?'

She drew the crumpled page of newsprint from the *Telegraph* files from her pocket. Not bearing to touch him, she dropped it on the carpet in front of him. He picked it up, studied the photograph of the New Year festivities in 1966 and then screwed it up in a tight ball in his fist.

'It's just you and me, Sheila, you and me.'

For a moment she didn't know what he meant and then she understood. In his tormented mind he was searching for a way out. But before her brain could take in the implications of his strange statement the telephone rang. She stared at it, disbelieving. For the past hour she'd been closeted in a private hell with her father. Now this shrill signal from the outside world seemed like a lifeline.

She reached eagerly for the phone, but Andrew Tracy got there first, clamping his large hand down on the receiver. 'Don't answer it.' He towered over her as the peals echoed round the room and finally stopped. 'You have to hear me out.'

I don't have to stay, she told herself. He'd never harm me, not even to save his life. All it would take were a few steps to the door. But she knew she hadn't the strength or the courage to take those few steps. She was trapped as surely as he was.

'None of this would have come out if it hadn't been for that boy, Harry Riley.' He seemed so sure that he could keep his secrets forever. How could he be so sure, she wondered. 'I'd heard he was digging around, seeing a lot of Nicholas. I even found out he was related to Bailey.'

'How you must have been laughing at me, trying to discover everything you already knew. Suspecting everyone but you,' she said bitterly.

'Not laughing. I was scared.'

'Harry had to die because you were scared. It wasn't even revenge. Revenge is a reason.' She couldn't trust herself to look at him.

But he was beyond any rationality like that. 'I did lie to you. Once. When he telephoned that day, Wednesday, he thought at first it was you who had answered. He started to say, "Sheila, I have to see you, you mustn't stay." Then he realized it was me and he put down the phone. I knew then that he'd managed to put together all the pieces. And if he hadn't it would just be a matter of time.'

'I learned when I called the office that he was going to the cinema in Brighton that night and followed him. I left when he left. I tailed him in the car to a quiet spot. He didn't even notice me. I took the car jack and . . . I don't think he felt anything. He just slumped to the ground. He was so little. I dragged him into the car. I didn't know what I meant to do. But then I found I'd driven to the cliff edge and it seemed too easy. You do see that, Sheila. I had no choice.

'I got out that flask of brandy I keep in the glove compartment and forced some down his lips. He gagged and seemed to come to. I remember his eyes, staring. He was looking at me as you're looking at me now. I had to stop him looking at me like that. I shoved him out of the car and he lay there, not moving, just staring. And the next thing I knew I'd pitched him over the cliff. I heard the sound of his body bumping against the rocks and that awful dull thud when it reached the bottom. I knew he was dead.'

He covered his face with his hands, a dry, rasping sob came from his throat. At last he looked up at her, waiting for her judgement. But she no longer recognized him. All she saw was a murderer.

CHAPTER 22

She'd lost track of time. Maybe it was an hour, maybe only a few minutes, before he broke the silence between them.

'What are you going to do?'

In the second before he asked she wouldn't have known what to reply. But in framing the question he'd crystallized the answer for her.

'You know very well. I have to call the police.' The dull resignation in her voice was beyond any plea for mercy or claim on filial loyalty.

'There's no proof.'

'Proof!' She couldn't believe that even now he was still play acting, convincing himself that he had some kind of immunity from retribution. 'When they know what they're looking for, they'll find proof. Do you think that cashier at the Palace couldn't identify you? Do you honestly imagine when the police start inquiring that no one will remember noticing you tailing Harry that night? They'll find proof. And to think I suspected Alec or George Lacey or Jack Murray or even old Edgar Blythe. That's what you've done to me. You talk about love. You couldn't have loved me.' A new, shivering thought struck her. 'You must have sent me that note: "Forget Harry Riley". I'm not your daughter. I'm just another of your victims.'

'I wanted to protect you,' he said brokenly.

'From what? From you!'

She observed his reactions to her words dispassionately. First the aching grief, then, momentarily, a kind of wounded frenzy, the human instinct for self-preservation at any cost.

'You can kill me if you like. I don't care. You've as good as killed me anyway,' she said, unmoved.

For a fleeting moment he stared at her, weighing her invitation. One murder is hard, two is easier, three . . . She watched him wrestling with the primeval urge to do away with the one person who could destroy him and the emotional bond between father and daughter. She saw the disintegration of this man who for so long had been the better part of her life and, strangely, felt no concern for her own safety. It was as if she were offering herself as a hostage to his fate.

Then the tension seeped out of him. The fine lion face relaxed, no longer distorted with anguish or fear. He looked at her serenely as he'd looked at her lovingly so often in the past. And she knew she'd won.

'I could never harm you, Sheila. You must do what you have to do.'

I can't hate him, she told herself wonderingly. Despite everything, I can't hate him.

The sudden, urgent knocking on the front door seemed almost an anti-climax. He made no move to stop her opening it.

'Sheila! Thank God.'

She felt Stephen Gough's arms around her and registered the distraught figure of Eleanor Rushton behind him. She gazed up at Stephen listlessly, her body and mind numb. She let him lead her back into the study and sit her gently in the chair by the roll-top desk with the photograph album open at the portrait of Sarah Rushton.

'How did you . . . ?' she managed to say. But before she could finish she realized that her part in the tragedy was over. It had been taken out of her hands by Eleanor Rushton, back where it started. And she felt an intruder.

'Why, Andrew, why?'

Where have I heard that before? thought Sheila. Then she remembered. It was me. It was me. She clutched Stephen's hand, not wanting to hear but knowing she must. There was no escape.

Her father was looking at Eleanor Rushton, his eyes pleading as they'd pleaded with Sheila.

'How could I have been so blind as not to see what you and Nicholas had done? Sarah was my daughter. I brought her up. I cared for her. If I could live with what happened to her, why couldn't you? That boy, Billy Stride, that poor man Bailey, Harry Riley!'

'I never wanted you to know.'

'And maybe I wouldn't have known, that's the disgusting thing, if it hadn't been for Sheila and Nicholas last night. I listened to his babbling on the phone to Sheila and then afterwards he told me everything. Only he was drunk and I couldn't bring myself to believe him. I tried to convince myself it was the alcohol talking. But then when Jimmy Grant and Stephen called I knew he'd been speaking the truth. Only he wasn't there any longer to confirm it. He was dead, too. I can almost forgive you for everything else, Andrew. But not for Nicholas. Why did you have to kill Nicholas? He was no good. But he didn't deserve to die.'

He'd listened to her, resigned and beaten, but as she accused him of murdering Nicholas, Andrew Tracy looked up at her in horror.

Sheila glanced at Stephen, questioningly. Hadn't George Lacey confessed to driving the car that killed Nicholas? Stephen shook his head quickly at her and tightened his grip on her hand.

She heard her father protesting weakly. 'I didn't. I couldn't do that to you. Ellie, you have to know that.'

She drew herself up at his use of a lover's name for her. In that instant she became proud Mrs Eleanor Rushton again, not the sad, bereaved woman who had stood on the doorstep.

'You always were a fool, Andrew,' she said cuttingly.

It was the final wound, more painful than anything Sheila had inflicted on him.

He looked around him from Eleanor to Stephen to Sheila, bewildered.

'I suppose I must go to the police.' His voice was steady now and he addressed himself to Sheila. 'I'll just get my coat.' Before he reached the door he turned. 'You'll look after her, Steve?' Stephen Gough nodded.

It wasn't cold and, as he left the room, Sheila noticed he was already wearing a heavy jacket.

'Steve . . .' she whispered and made to run after him. But Stephen pulled her back towards him.

'Don't, Sheila. He knows what he's doing.'

'Jimmy Grant. I have to phone . . .'

'Grant's around. I talked him into letting me do it my way when you didn't answer the phone.'

Eleanor Rushton picked up the album, studied the photograph of the young, vulnerable girl with her mother's eyes and snapped it shut sharply. There was an awful sound of finality as the pages clapped against each other.

'And you talked him into letting me think Andrew killed Nicholas, too, didn't you?'

Stephen sighed deeply. 'I'm sorry.'

'Sorry!' she said bitterly. 'Small word.'

'It was the only way we could get you . . . we could get at the truth.'

'I think I knew,' she admitted. 'I couldn't bear the burden of what Nicholas had told me any longer. Who . . . ?'

'It was George Lacey. Truly an accident.'

'Poor Nicholas. I never really liked him. He was my son. And I never really liked him. I suppose that's a dreadful confession.'

It wasn't the confession, it was the fact that Eleanor Rushton had felt forced to utter it that made Sheila pity her.

They heard the sound of a car revving up in the driveway and then backing recklessly into the road. Sheila twisted out of Stephen's grasp and rushed to the front door.

'Dad!' It was the first time she'd called him that since she'd learned how he'd deceived her all these years, but he was out of earshot.

'He won't get far,' said Stephen.

She looked into his eyes and knew that he was right.

The police found his body and the wrecked car at the bottom of the Seahaven cliff where Harry Riley had met his death a few nights before. At last, the two lives of Andrew Tracy were at peace.

CHAPTER 23

For two days she sat in her father's favourite chair staring out at the garden he'd taken such pride in tending. Not seeing, not hearing, refusing to go to bed or take more than the most meagre nourishment. Stephen Gough never left her side. Her doctor spoke of shock, grief and time healing everything. And though Stephen understood the sense of what he was saying, he resented the medical and moral platitudes.

He took the telephone calls and turned away the visitors and wondered how he could break through the silent barrier she'd erected around herself.

Then on the third morning the florist's boy arrived with a bouquet of late spring flowers. It was a poor little bouquet obviously from someone who hadn't much money to spend and the florist had taken little care in assembling it.

She looked at the limp blossoms and fingered the card that went with them without interest.

'Read it,' he urged her. She shook her head listlessly.

'Read it,' he repeated, more commandingly.

She took the card out of its envelope and gazed at the scrawled handwriting for a long time. Then he saw what he'd been waiting and hoping for. A tear trickled down her cheek, then another, followed by an avalanche of weeping that racked her body for several minutes. As she clung to him, he thanked God and whoever had sent those pathetic flowers.

Eventually the sobbing subsided and she handed the card to him. On it was inscribed simply: 'Thank you. Esther Bailey.'

It would still take time for her to fully confront the tragedy she must learn to live with, but it was a start.

Each day she grew stronger, more aware, more able to talk through the pain she was suffering and Stephen was always there to listen.

When she began to ask questions he knew she was on the road to recovery.

'The flowers? From Esther Bailey?'

'The case against her husband is going to be reopened. Eleanor Rushton has agreed to give evidence and . . .'

'Me.'

'That's up to you. It's your decision. No one would force you to testify against . . .'

'Andrew.' It was the first time she had referred to her father since she'd learned of his suicide. 'I must. I will. Otherwise it's all been wasted. It's all right, Steve. I can talk about him now. How did you suspect that he was involved?'

'Intuition.' He smiled. 'It's not just a woman's prerogative. When he spoke of Eleanor Rushton he talked like a man in love.'

'I never guessed.'

'I know. And I hoped I was wrong. But then when I spoke to Jimmy Grant about the Wednesday bridge night he told me that Andrew had opted out at the last moment. That's when we went to see Eleanor Rushton.'

'And all my suspicions. Alec, George, Jack Murray.'

'Murray had been helping Eleanor Rushton try to straighten out Nicholas. He's not such a bad sort, underneath all that bluster.'

'I'll never forgive myself. Oh Steve, what happens next? After Martin Bailey's cleared. Where do I begin to pick up the pieces? How can I face these people in Seahaven again?'

He put his hands on her shoulders and forced her to look at him. He noticed how thin she was, how worn the face that had always seemed so serene.

'You don't have to face them, Sheila. You owe them

nothing. There's a whole world outside Seahaven. And it's time you explored it. I'm taking you away from here.'

'You?'

'You don't think you're going to get rid of me now, do you?'

'But you've made your home here. You like it.'

'I did. Not any more. My home is with you. I don't promise things are going to be easy for you. You're going to have to learn to live with the fact that your father was a murderer. No, don't turn away. Listen to me. It will take a lot of courage. But maybe when you've got through that you can remember why you loved him, too. Maybe somehow you can come to terms with the schizophrenic life he led. You can do it. We can do it.'

She nodded, feeling his warmth flowing into her starved body. 'There's one thing I have to do, Steve. I'd like to see my half-sister, Sarah. Perhaps I can help her. Perhaps that's the legacy Andrew left me.'

He folded her tenderly in his arms. 'That's my girl.'

Outside the sun was shining on the town of Seahaven, people were going about their business, the *Telegraph* was preparing its next issue, council workmen were finally erecting a barrier on the cliff road and life went on.